BACK COVER

Trevor

After getting dumped, the last thing I need is to take on my advisor's niece as a new roommate. For starters, she's hot. Like, sexy librarian hot. But I need my advisor's recommendation for a job after graduation, so I'm going to keep my dirty little fantasies to myself... and stay far away from my sexy little roomie.

Natalie

I'm done with men. After my last dating disaster, I can't afford to get derailed again. So when my aunt claims to have found me the perfect roommate, I'm willing to give it a shot. He's one of my aunt's best students, so how distracting could he be?

Then Trevor opens the door to my new apartment, muscled, shirtless, tattooed, and so... arrogant. How can one guy be such a dick? He's bossy, and annoying...and scorching hot.

WANTON

M. MALONE
NANA MALONE

ALSO BY M. MALONE & NANA MALONE

- The Shameless Trilogy -

Shame (prequel)

Shameless / Shameful / UnAshamed

- The Force Duet -

Forcful (prequel)

Force / Enforce

- The Deep Duet -

In Deep (prequel)

Deep / Deeper

- The Sin Duet -

Beyond Sin (prequel)

Sin / Sinful

1

____

6 Weeks Ago...

I turned on the lights in my apartment and threw my keys in the small bowl on the entryway table. I sighed. It had been a long day, and I still had about three hours of studying left to do. But at least I could do it at home with Courtney. I was tired of being in the library, surrounded by all the other students who looked as manic about exams as I felt.

"Court? Are you here?"

It was dark in the back, so she must not have gotten home yet. That was strange. Courtney worked part-time at the bookstore, but she never worked this late, not even on nights when they were restocking. I checked my phone, making sure I hadn't missed a text from her. While scrolling absently through my messages, I walked into the kitchen, and pulled open the refrigerator for a bottle of water.

When I closed it, my eyes remained glued to the door. There was a note attached with a magnet.

My throat went dry as I recognized Courtney's distinctive loopy handwriting. She always curled her r's in a dramatic way and looped her j's, g's, and y's. My mind was stuck on those inconsequential things as I started to read.

Dear Trevor,

I know it's a cowardly thing to leave a note behind instead of facing you. Maybe I am a coward, but this was the only way I could tell you without chickening out. So here it is.

I'm not happy. God, I feel like such a bitch, but I've tried for two years to make it work and I just can't. I love you so much, but every day we grow farther apart. I don't want to drag this out until we hate each other. We want different things and that's okay.

I wish you nothing but the best.

Love,

Courtney

I held the note carefully as I read it again and again. My

mind was trying to find something in her words to explain how I could feel so blindsided. When I looked up, the room was slightly blurry, and I couldn't figure out why until a tear fell onto the paper.

I swiped my damp cheeks and crumpled the paper in my fist. Suddenly, I saw myself going on about the rest of my evening, heating up some dinner, studying until the wee hours, only to wake in the morning and do it all over again. Maybe I hadn't been the best boyfriend. Working long hours at the bar, coupled with a grueling school schedule, didn't leave a lot of time for being a romantic. But I'd thought that Courtney got it and supported me. Instead, based on that letter, she'd just been tolerating me for the past two years.

Anger replaced grief, and I pulled out my phone. What was I going to do, call her and scream? Yell? So we could have another fight just like all the others we'd had over the past few months? She'd always leave in a rage and stay out late deliberately to provoke me. Lately, she had been so different. Distant. I'd even started to think she was cheating on me.

My phone vibrated with a text. My heart lifted, until I saw that it wasn't Courtney. It was my sister, Talia.

Arrived on campus. TTYL

Thinking of my little sister always could make me smile, even when everything else in my life was shit. I couldn't call her right now. She'd be able to tell something was wrong. But thinking of her made me remember another phone call I needed to make.

As if I'd conjured it, my phone rang. When I saw my best friend Cage's name on the screen, I shook my head. Exactly who I wanted to talk to. Before I could even say hello, Cage was talking.

"Dude, you were right about Jenna. She just had another fucking tantrum about the L.A. thing. This time, she hit me in the ear with a shoe, and accused me of cheating just because I didn't do what she wanted and move with her."

Under other circumstances, I would have found the situation hilarious. I forced a laugh, since my friend would be expecting it. I'd tried to warn Cage about screwing around with those crazy chicks. I'd always told him to look for the more sensible types, like Courtney. Look at how that had turned out. Oddly, my friend's situation did make me feel a little better. I wasn't the only one going through shit, at least.

"I won't say I told you so. But only because I'm so happy you finally ditched her. She was hot, but no sex is worth dealing with that bullshit."

"I agree. So I'm going home to my apartment. The one I still have, thanks to you. I totally owe you for talking me out of moving in with her."

"You do owe me one. And I'm going to collect soon." I took a deep breath. "Remember my sister, Talia? It's been years since you've seen her."

"Of course."

"Well, she's transferring to NYU this year because they have the program she wants. I need you to keep an eye on her."

Cage was quiet. I hung my head. I knew this was going to be a hard sell. My friend liked to party, and babysitting someone as studious as Talia wouldn't exactly be a fun time for him.

"I thought Talia was a straight-A student in high school? Why would you be worried about her flunking out of college?"

"It's obvious you don't have sisters. I'm not worried about her flunking, genius. She's not like us. Talia will ace all of her classes without even trying."

"Okay, well then, what do you need me to do? I'm sure she doesn't need my help studying."

I made a face, glad my friend couldn't see me. Maybe it was just because I was in a bad mood already, but damn if it didn't seem like Cage was deliberately misunderstanding me.

"I need you to make sure no one bothers her. Help her get to her classes and shit. She's shy and has never made friends easily. If I was there, I could look out for her and make sure she doesn't spend the entire year in her room with her textbooks. But since I'm not, I'm counting on you to make sure she has some fun, but stays away from the wrong crowd."

Perhaps Cage finally heard the frustration in my voice, because when he spoke next, his voice had lost the attitude and sounded resigned.

"You got it, man. I'll show her around and make sure she knows where everything is. Hell, I know some goody-two-shoes girl types. Maybe I can introduce her to some friends."

I smiled. "Thank you. I've been really worried about this. I just want her to have a good time. She's always been so serious. I don't want her to study non-stop and never have any fun."

"You know I've got this. She'll have fun with me. Trust me."

I hung up, changing my mind about confiding in Cage. Surely, this was just some kind of temporary insanity from studying too hard for finals. Courtney was pre-med, and she'd been struggling with a few of her classes this semester. My friend had never liked Courtney, and if we ended up getting back together, I didn't want Cage reminding me of this.

In the meantime, though, I needed to be practical about how to pay the rent. On a whim, I pulled up the university Facebook page and posted a message about seeking a roommate. To my shock, I got a private message almost immediately from my advisor.

My niece just transferred in and she's looking for a place to stay.

2

———

6 weeks later...

N atalie! I'm so glad you're here, my dear girl."

I was immediately swept up into a hug that reminded me of summertime and long hours spent baking together. I pulled back slightly and regarded the older woman currently strangling me with love. My Aunt Patricia was still the most stylish woman I knew, even in her early sixties, and she *still* smelled like lemons and sugar.

I soaked up the love and comfort of my Aunt like a flower seeking sunlight. After the events of the past semester, I felt like I was just coming out of the dark.

Fucking Brian, I thought bitterly. Why was it that beautiful men were such liars? I'd swallowed all of his lines without even a thought, especially the worst lie of them all: that we'd go public with our relationship as soon as I wasn't his student anymore. After I'd finished the class, he'd simply made up another excuse: that he was worried about the backlash because I was still a student at the university.

I wished I'd wised up on my own and seen through his charade, but I hadn't. Instead, I'd overheard another student crying over her boyfriend, the handsome chemistry TA named Brian. But at least I could say that once I'd seen the light, I'd acted quickly. Brian had claimed he didn't know the girl, or that I must have misunderstood. But once the wool has been pulled from your eyes, it's extraordinarily hard to put it back.

Plus, Brian wasn't as great of a liar as he thought he was. When I'd first told him what happened, I'd seen the fear in his eyes.

So, with a broken heart and completely smashed sense of trust, I'd put in for a transfer to Boston University. My Aunt Patty had taught in the information technology department at the university for the past ten years. It made me sad to leave Florida State behind, because I loved my school. The thought still made me a little grumpy. It wasn't the school's fault that they employed manipulative bastards.

"Hi, Aunt Patty. Sorry it took me so long to get here. Traffic was terrible."

My Aunt waved away my excuses with a manicured hand. "It's no trouble at all. I have your key and directions right here, just in case Trevor isn't home when you get there."

It was the first time my Aunt had referred to my new room-mate by name. I was still surprised my aunt was okay with me rooming with a guy. When I'd mentioned it, Aunt Patty had just chuckled and said, "He's not your type at all. Besides, he won't even notice you're there unless you speak in CSS."

I figured out later that was some kind of computer code. My Aunt knew that I'd always gone more for the jock type. Growing up, I'd been way more inclined to talk to my aunt about boys than my own mother.

"Thanks again for finding me a place. I never would have had time after dealing with all the transfer stuff."

Aunt Patty took my bag and placed it on the sofa. "Come have a cup of tea first. Sorry your Uncle Sidney isn't here to greet you. He had a class he couldn't cancel."

"It's no problem. Once I'm settled in, we'll have to go out for dinner."

After an hour relaxing over tea, I set out for my new apartment with my aunt's list of detailed instructions and my new set of house keys. I felt a little tingle of excitement as I parked in space 601, per the written instructions, and grabbed my largest suitcase from my trunk. It hit me then that I should probably carry my least valuable things up first, so they weren't sitting in the hallway. Luckily, I didn't have much since there was no elevator. One big box, three smaller ones, and two suitcases. It took me five trips up and down the stairs before I got it all.

Afterward, I leaned against the wall outside my new apartment, panting. It might have been a bad idea to do all that alone, but I really didn't want to start my relationship with my roommate by asking him for help. I wasn't sure what strings my aunt had pulled to get this guy to agree to let me move in. If he was some kind of geeky computer nerd, then he probably was worried about having some party girl move in. So I was planning to be the best roommate ever. Easy. Quiet. He wouldn't even know I was there.

I knocked once. The door swung open after a few minutes. The guy who stood in the doorway stared at me.

I stared back.

I could feel the moment my mouth fell open, but was powerless to stop it. This was my new roommate? My eyes scanned over him from head to toe, too overwhelmed to know what to take in first. The wild, dark hair that stood out randomly, like he'd just gotten out of bed, the chiseled jawline, or the moody green eyes currently watching me like I was prey.

Or the abs. Dear Lord, the abs. He had more dips and cuts in his stomach than I even knew was possible. Was that an eight pack?

At the last moment, I pulled my eyes back up to his face. But by his smirk, I knew he'd caught me staring. The beginnings of a blush heated my cheeks. Damn, I hated how easy it was to make me blush. I always wanted to act cool and confident, but that was pretty much impossible when my red cheeks gave me away.

Oh, you're sexy as hell? No big deal, new roommate. I've totally lived with lots of half-naked sexy men before.

Right.

Resisting the urge to check if my dark hair was still contained in my usual ponytail, I gave an awkward little wave.

"Hi, I'm Natalie. I'm your new roommate."

———

I WAS FUCKED.

There was no other way to put it. Just fucked.

I knew it the moment I'd opened the door. If this girl was what Professor Washington meant by mousy and quiet, then we had entirely different definitions of what mousy was. It also didn't help that she stared at me like I was a Christmas turkey and she hadn't eaten in years. Her big cornflower-blue eyes went wide and her pupils dilated

Focus, man. Now is not the time. My advisor had asked me for a favor. And, as she was helping me to find a job, I needed to get this favor right.

Besides, it would be a recipe for disaster if I started fantasizing about my new roommate. So I'd just have to shove the mental image of her full lips completely out of my head.

"Do you need a hand with anything?" I asked. Maybe if I had something to do with my hands, I wouldn't think about running them over every inch of her body. And through that thick chestnut hair, gently massaging her scalp as I angled her head to kiss her. *No. None of that.* "Here, let me grab that box."

"Thank you. I, uh—I really appreciate you doing this last

minute. Letting me come and live with you. Seriously, are you some kind of saint?"

A saint? No. I was far from that. "Hardly. But I know what it's like trying to find an apartment in the city. Come on in." I grabbed one of the boxes and hauled it into the living room. Jesus, what the hell did she have in there? The way it jostled, I assumed books. But I couldn't be sure.

She dragged one of the suitcases just inside the door, and then took a look around. The apartment wasn't that big. But it had a spare bedroom, hardwood floors, was rent-controlled, and clean. I was a bit of a design nut, so the furnishings, while secondhand, were still stylish and eclectic. I'd been able to find cheap knockoff versions of the stuff I saw in magazines. Maybe it was my analytical mind, but I really liked smooth, clean lines.

Did she like it? Suddenly, it really mattered to me what she thought of the place. I wanted her to be comfortable here. It shouldn't matter what anyone thought, but I found myself wanting to make a good first impression.

"This is really great. I had no idea what I was going to be getting, but this is nice."

A grin tugged at my lips. I'd been lucky to get this place at all, right in the heart of Brighton, of all places. I'd worked hard on his place and would almost be sad to leave it. But I'd be moving on to bigger and better things soon.

I had only gotten the apartment because one of the guys in my major had landed a big flashy job in Silicon Valley, and had asked me to take over the lease. That was probably how that guy had gotten the apartment, too.

This place had probably passed through a slew of grad students passing it off to people they knew and liked. It was the way of things. In the crazy world of Boston real estate, you had to have an in to find a place to live.

"Your bedroom's through there. You have your own shower. This is the common area. Not huge, but not totally cramped either. You're pretty much standing in the kitchen and dining room area. My room's back that way." I inclined my head toward the opposite side of the hallway.

As I helped to pull the rest of her things into the apartment, I couldn't help but feel her hot stare on my back. I considered grabbing a shirt and putting it on, but fuck it. I kind of liked her looking. Her eyes were striking, even more striking when they were intensely focused on me.

You are asking for trouble. Yeah, but I didn't care. Because I was sneaking glances of my own.

She had the whole studious-student get up going. Basic jeans, simple top. Cardigan and the glasses perched atop her head. I had the feeling she maybe needed them for reading, instead of for walking around and shit. The damned things would likely give me sexy librarian fantasies.

Stop with the fantasies.

Problem was, once my brain had already started on that line of thinking, I couldn't help it. Those tits of hers were hard to hide under the soft cotton fabric. Seriously though, how the hell was I supposed to focus?

One of the boxes tipped over, and I caught it just before the contents came spilling out. When I looked inside, I grinned. "Oh my God, is this what I think it is?"

She flushed and made to grab it, but I quickly snatched it out of her reach, and kept digging through the box. "Is this *Maximum Death*? Oh my God. Tell me this isn't *Marked for Death*?"

Natalie folded her arms right under that impressive chest. "So? I like bad action movies. When I need to unwind and relax, and get my mind off of whatever is bothering me, I watch one of those because they're just so absurd. Are you judging me now?"

"Are you kidding? I love action movies. Pretty much anything with an explosion or gunfight, and I'm happy." She narrowed her eyes as if she wasn't sure if I was making fun of her not. I continued and teased her. "Matter-of-fact, I'm not even sure that you're a real fan."

"Are you insane? Anything with Van Damme or Segal, and I'm there. I love the ones when, you know, the lone random guy goes to some country, usually China, and the locals take him in, and teach him their secret arts, and then he becomes the great white hope. They're so bad."

I chuckled. "Ahh, I see my new roommate likes the classics."

"Is there really any other way to go?"

I helped her drag the last of her boxes into her bedroom. I was pretty much ready to leave her to sort things out. But then her gaze flickered to my chest again, and I couldn't help the smirk that played across my lips.

She shifted her gaze away quickly. "Uhm, I'm sorry, but you mind putting on a shirt? It's a little distracting."

Distracting? So she liked what she saw. *Not that it should matter to you, because you can't have her.* My dick had other ideas about that. But I wasn't listening to my dick right now, even if I wanted to.

"I have a list of house rules. Actually, only one, really: 'My house my rules.' Feel free to walk around shirtless yourself. I promise you, I won't mind."

Okay perfect, I was being a dick to my new roommate. But the frustration was already eating at me. Just knowing that I was going to be living with her was gnawing at my control. Which was even more annoying.

I was that guy, the one who never let anything slip. Never had one toe out of line, never once slipped up. Oh, I had fun. But I kept lines nice and clear, with good, proper boundaries, so there was never any confusion or question later.

Doing the kind of things that were running through my mind with my roommate would result in all kinds of blurry gray lines. And I didn't like that.

"So, I just have to deal?" she asked.

I nodded. "Yep. Welcome to the neighborhood, roomie." And then got the hell out of Dodge. One more minute closed in her bedroom with her, and my dick was going to start taking over my mind.

And that would be a very, very bad thing.

3

I stared at the search results for the best local bars and hangout spots. The last thing on earth I wanted to do was to go out to a bar by myself. But as I was in a new city, with no friends of my own just yet, I had no choice but to put myself out there.

I peered at the list of places. The three that were closest to the apartment were all highly rated by sassy-looking twenty-something women saying things like, "*Great drinks! Awesome music. Cute bartenders.*"

I couldn't be mad at cute bartenders, could I?

The problem was, the more I stared at the listings, the more my anxiety threatened to take over. Not that I was anti-people or extremely shy--okay, maybe I was a little shy. But this was fine. I could do this. It was more that I was walking into a brand-new situation, and I didn't know how to go about it. For a long time, I'd depended so much on my ex, Brian, but I hadn't even realized it.

My friends had been his friends. From the time we met, we just about did everything together. So for a long time, I'd never had to experience anything new alone. And that was bad.

Get off your ass, put on some skinny jeans and a cleavage-baring top, and go. Yes. Sexy top, check. Skinny jeans, check. Heels that I only ever wore to go out, check. Makeup done, hair fluffed.

When I looked at myself in the mirror, I barely recognized myself. I hardly ever wore my contacts. But going out with glasses was never something I enjoyed. And glasses often got in the way of kissing. Not that I planned to make out with anyone, but still. There was always hope. *Is there really?*

I shoved aside that thought. I was trying new things. And that meant going out on my own. It meant meeting new people.

With my clutch in hand, I walked the three blocks to the bar. Thankfully, it was still late summer, so the evening was balmy and warm, the last vestiges of the August heat holding on tightly and refusing to give way to fall.

When I walked up to the bar, the guy at the door immediately stuck his palm out for my ID.

Even though I was twenty-one, I was well aware that I looked about sixteen. I handed it over gladly and peered inside.

As promised, the bar was hopping. But it wasn't too crowded yet, since it was only about 7:30. I'd missed most of the happy hour crowd, and it was still too early for the pregame crowd. But there were people dancing, friends crowded around tables and laughing. And from the brightly colored drink concoctions in front of people, it looked like the cocktails were flowing.

I took my ID back from the bouncer at the door, and he gave me a wide smile.

"Have fun." His eyes crinkled at the corners, and I realized that he had a nice smile. Then he winked at me. It was hard not to wonder how many pretty girls he'd winked at so far since his shift started.

"I think I will."

I opened the door and glanced around, looking for a table. I didn't want to look like too much of a loser by taking one of the big tables by myself, so instead I opted to meander toward the bar, and was quite happy to find a barstool open near the end.

The girl I sat next to smiled at me warmly. "You need to try the watermelon martini. It's awesome."

I grinned at her. "Thanks. I think I will."

I glanced down the bar and searched for a bartender. There were two of them. One was shorter and stockier, with a sleeve of tattoos peeking out from under his short sleeve shirt. He had hands like meat cleavers. But even with his thick fingers, he handled each of the drinks delicately.

The other one was tall. Very tall. Broad shoulders. I could see a tattoo or two peeking out from his short sleeve shirt. He also made my mouth water a little, and I hadn't even seen his face.

Yeah, but you've seen what those jeans do for his ass, and ... Yeah, okay. No way a guy looked like that from the back and wasn't hot from the front. That would just be some sort of cruel, karmic joke.

The stocky guy caught my eye first, and came down to my end of the bar. "What can I get you, beautiful?" He had a thick Boston accent that instantly made me smile.

I nodded to my new friend's drink. "Whatever in the world that watermelon thing is."

"You got it." When he went to grab a glass, the other bartender turned around, and my heart caught in my throat.

Oh, shit. Trevor.

Of course that would be Trevor. Because apparently, I couldn't get away from him, his abs, that smile, and Jesus Christ, those eyes. Were green eyes that color even natural? It would really help if I thought they were contacts or something.

At the other end of the bar, he smiled and flirted with some other girl. Blonde. Of course, he probably preferred blondes. Which was just fine by me. Not that I cared.

As if he could feel my gaze on him, his head swiveled and our eyes met. He blinked in surprise, and a small smile tugged at his lips.

Oh, great. Now it would be awkward. Like, he would be forced to talk to me, or something. I mustered a light wave, and he nodded then turned to the other bartender and said something in his ear. The guy's gaze immediately flickered over to me, then back to Trevor. Then he shrugged. He handed the drink he was making over to Trevor.

What in the world was happening? A few minutes later, Trevor sauntered down to my end of the bar. "Here's your drink. I call it the Ladies' Orgasm."

The corners of my lips twitched. "Are you sure that's what it's called?"

He grinned. "I had it made for you special."

I glared at it. "But I really wanted the watermelon drink."

"If it makes you feel better, I put watermelon liqueur in it." He grinned. "Try it. If you don't like it, I'll bring you the drink on the menu."

I eyed the concoction, not sure if I should trust him or not. But when I took a sip, I had to admit it was delicious. Problem was, I couldn't taste the alcohol at all. Which worried me. Because that meant I would more than likely have one hell of a hangover tomorrow. "You're right. It's good."

He winked at me. "You can say I know my way around a woman's orgasm." And then he sauntered off.

Jackass. He was incorrigible. He was deliberately teasing me. Trying hard to be outrageous. Well, it would take a lot more of these drinks for me to sweat.

The girl on the stool next to me leaned over. "Oh my God, you have the bartender flirting with you and making personalized drinks? You're a girl I definitely need to know. I'm Lila."

I stuck out my hand. "Natalie. Nice to meet you."

For the next twenty minutes, as I sipped my drink, my new friend introduced me to everyone she was with. And just like that, I had a hodgepodge group of people that I sort of knew.

The next drink Trevor brought over was called a Lick and a Promise. Again, I couldn't taste the alcohol at all. Jesus, how was he making these drinks? But again, I sipped happily as I chatted with my new friends. The alcohol loosened me up, so I wasn't my usual shy and uptight self.

The next drink he brought me, he called a Dick Lick. At this point, I was pretty sure he was making up the names. But Lila assured me that those were real drinks.

After the next sexually suggestive drink he brought over, I was getting loose. Happy.

From the end of the bar, as he made drinks, I could always feel Trevor kind of checking in on me. Occasionally nodding with his eyebrows raised, as if to ask if I was okay. I returned the looks with a happy smile. I wished I could pretend I wasn't attracted to him. But honestly, who wouldn't be attracted to him?

He had the face of a freaking model. And the body of, well, it was better if I didn't think about his body. But too late. There it was. The throbbing between my thighs that had started the second he'd opened the door shirtless refused to go away.

It looked like my battery-operated boyfriend was going to be getting a hell of a lot of use this year.

I had a feeling that, with a face like that, he slept with a lot of girls. He probably didn't keep too many of them around for very long. Plus, they all probably looked like models, not hyper-nerdy psychology students.

One of Lila's friends, Matt, asked me to dance, and usually, I would've said no. But I was already feeling all the good vibes from the alcohol, so I said yes. It was some kind of hip-hop mix, with totally recognizable radio tracks. And I loved it.

Well, I loved it at first.

Everything was going great. I even had a little rhythm. I wouldn't be in a music video or anything, but I could stay on beat. And I didn't look like an awkward chicken flailing my arms everywhere. Everything was great, until Matt started to slide his hand over my hips to my ass. I shifted out of his grip and shook my head.

"Easy on the hands."

"Well, how else do you expect to dance?"

"We've been doing just fine without your hands on my ass."

From my peripheral vision, I could see Trevor watching us, his gaze boring in on the side of my face. Matt tried to pull me closer again, and leaned his face in. But I just moved back, wanting out of his reach.

"Dude, still too close."

He threw his hands up. "What the hell is wrong with you? You're the one who's been drunk and flirting with me all night."

Had I been flirting with him? I was so out of practice. I thought she was just being nice. "You know what, I think I'm done."

But before I could get away, he snapped his hand around my wrist and tried to pull me back. "No, I think we should finish the dance."

I tugged my wrist loose, and rubbed it gently where he'd gripped too hard. "And I said no thank you."

I turned to move back through the crowd, but my face planted into a rock hard chest. Irritated, I craned my head up to find Trevor standing there with a scowl on his face. He was glaring directly at Matt.

"That's enough. Door's that way. You should probably hit the skids."

Matt frowned. "What the fuck? She was the one that was grinding all over me."

Trevor shook his head. "From the looks of it, she doesn't feel like dancing anymore. Time for you to take the hint."

Matt glared at me, but he eventually just flipped me off, and headed back through the crowd toward the door.

"Thanks for that. But you didn't need to."

"Yeah, I did. If the bouncers had come over, it would've been a whole thing. You okay?"

"I'm fine. I guess maybe I was flirting with him. I think I had too much to drink."

His lips tipped into a wry smile. "Actually, I've been sending you virgin drinks all night."

I blinked up at him. "What? Those drinks were all virgin?"

He nodded and shrugged. "Well, I didn't see you come in with any friends. So I was looking out for you."

A hot wash of embarrassment flooded over me. "So, I *have* been flirting with him and just chatting away like an idiot? And I can't even blame alcohol? Great."

"I don't see what you're so upset about. You seemed perfectly fine. And I wanted to make sure that your inhibitions stayed intact. You don't seem the type to go to a bar by yourself."

"What? So you think you were helping me?"

"I'm your roommate. I was just trying to look out for you."

I couldn't believe it. More than anything, the embarrassment was going to kill me. I shoved away from him. "I'm going home." I heard him call my name, but I just grabbed my purse and headed straight for the door. Maybe this whole "making friends and trying new things" idea had been a mistake.

By then, my feet were killing me, so I just took a cab three blocks back to the apartment. Within thirty minutes, I had my makeup off and was in my comfy pajamas, snuggled in my bed. I was still awake when Trevor came home an hour later, and I lay perfectly still.

I told myself I wasn't listening to see if he'd come home with anyone. After all, that was none of my business. But I was lying to myself. I was desperate to know.

And I was still stinging from the embarrassment of how I'd acted tonight. The one thing that struck me, though, was that I'd been perfectly chatty and friendly without the assistance of alcohol. As a psychology student, I knew the effect well: *the placebo effect*. I'd thought I had a little alcoholic assistance, so I'd felt more comfortable. But it was still embarrassing to know what he'd done.

Within ten minutes, I heard Trevor's shower going, and I tried to relax and force myself to sleep. Tomorrow was another day. But that's when I heard it. The moan.

The long, slow, drawn out sound that made my clit pulse. The kind of sound that guys made when they were—oh my God. Had he actually brought someone home after all? No. I would've heard it. So what was he doing in there?

Never mind. It didn't take a genius to figure it out as I heard his low, soft curse. He was—uh—taking care of business. But the real question was, just who was he thinking about?

4

———

Just what the hell was so funny?

I paced back and forth in the kitchen. Originally, I'd come in here to get a cup of coffee that I hoped would keep me awake. I'd worked late the prior night, and had almost overslept this morning for class. But all the fatigue I'd been fighting all day evaporated when I saw Natalie with that guy. Alex, she'd called him.

She'd brought a guy home.

Why does it matter? I gritted my teeth. It shouldn't make a damn bit of difference who she brought home. But somehow, it did. Over the last week, I'd been in a state of constant anxiety. As much as I tried to avoid her, Natalie was *everywhere*.

Her strawberries and cream scent was in every room. Her shoes were by the front door, kicked off casually next to my favorite pair of hiking boots. Her ass was right there, in criminally tight jeans, whenever I came out of my room. The shower had become my only refuge, and I'd resorted to jacking off several times each night, just to take the edge off.

Not that it helped. Natalie was there, too. She'd left a bottle of her shampoo under the sink next to my bar soap the last time her water had run cold. Thanks to the addition done on this unit ten years ago, the two bathrooms ran on different water lines.

On the ledge of the tub, she'd placed her travel bottle of shower gel, which I'd discovered with delight was the source of her mouth-watering scent.

And yes, I'd jacked off while smelling it. *Don't judge.*

More laughter floated in from the living room, and I couldn't take it anymore. My jealousy was foolish; I knew that. My rational mind even knew that Natalie probably wasn't trying to tease me by wearing such tight jeans and smelling so edible. But on another level, I suspected she knew exactly what she did to me with those shy smiles and longing glances of hers. Oh, yes, I'd caught her staring *many* times.

She might pretend to be innocent, but the little vixen knew she was driving me insane, and enjoyed it.

Well, no more.

If she wanted to bring guys home and flaunt them in my face, then I could do it, too. I sent a text to my friend Jenny. She was a sophomore programming major, and had asked me to tutor her. I'd told her I didn't have time, but, hell, I could make time. I wasn't just going to sit in here like a loser.

About ten minutes later, I heard a knock on the front door. I smiled.

Natalie appeared at the entrance to the kitchen. Her eyes narrowed. "You have a guest."

Jenny walked around her, giving Natalie a curious look. "Trevor, you didn't tell me you had a sister."

Natalie snorted. "I'm not his sister. I'm his new roommate."

Jenny shrugged. "Oh. Cool. Nice to meet you."

I opened the fridge and got out a bottle of water, and offered it to Jenny. She took it while looking uncertainly between me and Natalie.

"Nice to meet you, too." Natalie's eyes slid to mine before she turned around and left.

Jenny wrapped her arms around my neck. "I'm glad you called. I could use a little stress relief." She licked her lips.

Nothing.

I glanced down at my dick in disbelief. What the hell? Not even a twitch? Jenny was gorgeous in a rock-chick kind of way, with spiky, jet-black hair, and dark eyes that she rimmed with a ton of black eye shadow. And that mouth? *Jesus.* Usually just the thought of those pillowy lips could get me hard.

Today, nothing.

"Let's go to my room."

Jenny's eyes lit up in excitement. She grabbed my hand and followed as I led her from the kitchen to the living room. Natalie didn't even look up, but the guy she was with watched us closely, his eyes locked on Jenny.

The fucker couldn't even keep from ogling other women while he was sitting right next to Natalie. I scowled at him until he turned away. Was that the kind of guy she liked?

Once we reached my room, Jenny was all over me, her hands diving into my hair as she tried to climb me. I gently tugged her hands down and stepped back.

Jenny frowned. "What's the matter? I thought this was why you asked me to come over."

"I texted you so we could work on your database design. You said you needed help, remember?"

She rolled her eyes. "I just said that because I wanted a reason to hang out. I figured you knew that." She tucked a finger into the front of my jeans, brushing the skin on my lower abdomen.

I gulped. This was about to get embarrassing, or awkward. I was totally not into this, and it wasn't going to take long before that fact was physically apparent.

"Let's watch a movie, then. Get to know each other a little," I added hurriedly when Jenny narrowed her eyes.

"Okay. That's really nice, actually. It's nice to meet a guy who wants to get to know me." Jenny settled on the bed, and I took the other side.

For the next hour, we watched a romantic comedy that made me want to gouge my eyes out. The soundtrack was punctuated by the occasional peal of laughter from the living room. I groaned. Now they were just being obnoxious. *Nothing* was that funny.

Just then, the sound of Natalie's voice floated from the living room, followed by deep, masculine laughter. I couldn't tell exactly what they were saying, but tried to listen anyway. *Ha ha... believe it... ha ha... some women are scared of cock.*

Wait, what? I pushed past Jenny, and flung open the door to my room. Before I could think about it, I stormed down the hall and into the living room. Natalie and Alex both turned to stare at me when my foot banged into the edge of the side table.

"Fuck," I muttered.

Jenny appeared at my side. "Are you okay?"

I clamped my lips together and nodded. There was no way I would admit how much that had hurt.

Suddenly, Jenny looked at her wrist. "Crap, I have to go. I'll call you later, okay?" She grabbed me around the waist and hugged me. "I had fun."

"Me too." I walked her to the door. When I got back to the living room, my toe was only throbbing a little.

"Everything okay?" Alex asked.

I ignored him. "What have you guys been doing out here? It sounded like... well, never mind that."

Natalie stood, and Alex did as well, stooping to pick up a black backpack from his feet.

"So I'll see you tomorrow, okay?"

"Bright and early," Natalie responded.

Alex kissed her on the forehead and then passed by me, brushing up against me. "Nice tats," he whispered.

I backed up, startled by the intimate tone in the man's voice. I glanced over at Natalie, who was already sitting down again, scribbling something in her notebook.

I put on a strained smile as I met Alex's eyes. "Thanks, I guess."

Alex leaned closer. "I left my number on your whiteboard. I'd love to see how far down those tats go."

Alex winked and then walked out of the room. A few seconds later, the front door closed.

5

———

I knew I should let it go.

But I just couldn't help myself. He'd spent the whole damn night trying to ruin my study session. For what? For the most part, as a roommate, he was fine. But there was always an aloofness to him, as if he didn't want me there, or didn't want to talk to me. He wasn't unfriendly, but we weren't friends. And he'd made that perfectly clear. When I found him in the kitchen, I couldn't resist poking the bear just a little bit. "So, how was your study session?"

Trevor looked up from the dishes he was cleaning in the sink to glare at me. "My study session was just fine. How was yours? I don't imagine you got much studying done, since you were talking about cocks all the time."

I couldn't help but laugh. "Exactly what do you think I was studying?"

"Well, clearly you were too busy flirting with your new boyfriend." He turned his attention back to the dishes in the sink. "You can do better. You know that right?"

"What business is it of yours?"

"Look, it's not my business who you date. But, you know, since we're roommates and all, I do sort of feel the need to warn you. As a boyfriend, that Alex dude sucks."

I was having fun with this. I crossed my arms and leaned back against the counter. "Oh, yeah? Why's that?"

"Well for starters, the jackass hit on me. He's totally batting for both teams. If that's what you're into, I don't care. But that's a douchebag move to hit on someone when you're with your girlfriend. No matter who you bat for."

I blinked at him. Then laughter tumbled out so hard that no sound followed. "Oh my God. You should see your face right now. All righteous indignation." More laughing. More clutching my sides. "Oh my God, this is just perfect."

He turned the water off, then turned to glare at me. "Just what the fuck is so funny?" He shook his head. "Whatever, you guys have an open relationship, that's your business. I thought I was doing the decent thing by telling you."

I wiped the tears of laughter from the corner of my eyes. "Trevor. I don't even know where to begin. But you should probably know, Alex doesn't like girls."

He frowned. "What the fuck are you talking about? That guy was all over you," he growled.

"No, he wasn't."

"Yes, he was. For fuck's sake, you were talking about sex. And cocks."

"You realize that we were discussing our sexual dysfunction paper. I'm a psych major, remember?"

His brows furrowed. "You think this is funny?"

I grinned, even as I pushed up my glasses. "Yeah, I kinda do. You're acting ridiculous. Hell, you're acting like a jealous boyfriend. What is your deal? You don't even like me."

His eyes darkened from emerald green to a rich moss color as he stared at me. Then, in the next second, he closed the distance between us, and bracketed me against the counter with his hands. "You're right. I *don't* like you."

Before I knew it, before I could even respond, before I could even mentally prepare, his lips were crushing mine.

First revelation, Trevor Hamilton could kiss. Not just like oh, "the guy was a good kisser", but like he should give lessons. He could hold seminars all about the art of it. The course would detail how much time to take. There would be bullets about the slide of the tongue, the pressure of the lips. Each course should be at least a weeklong seminar. Required coursework for all guys.

After the initial crush of his lips, he softened, gentled. He teased, probed, waited for me to respond, waited for me to allow him in. He had a subtle way of flooding the senses. He melted my resistance away, as if there had been any to begin with. My body slowly started melting, leaning into him, wanting more, craving more.

Before I knew it, my hands were sliding up to his pecs, and I was clutching onto his T-shirt. Under the soft cotton, he was all hard muscle and carved stone. When my nails dug in a little, he growled low and shoved one hand into my hair, gripping and angling my head just how he wanted as he took long licks into my mouth. Leaving no corner unexplored.

His body pressed into mine, forcing me to arch my back, if I didn't want it pressed into the edge of the counter. Of course, that motion made my breasts press against him more. My nipples were tight, my skin too hot. And, Jesus Christ, I could feel the thick length of him throbbing against my belly, as if claiming me. As if letting me know we were just getting started.

With another muffled groan, he lifted me on top of the counter so that his steel-like erection pressed against my center. Pressing into that spot I desperately needed the most.

Tomorrow, I would rethink this whole kissing situation, and have the wherewithal to be embarrassed. Tomorrow, I would look back on this and wonder what the hell I was thinking. Tomorrow, I would vow to never, ever do this with him again. Right now? Well, right now, I couldn't help it. Because he was kissing me like I'd never been kissed before. It was like he was reaching deep inside me, stroking every single pleasure center simultaneously.

The worst part was, he knew he was good. He would make little teasing licks and act as if he was withdrawing. And then I'd whimper, or instinctively follow the source of my pleasure, and he would give a muffled chuckle before delving in for more.

Before I even knew what the hell was happening, I felt a

tingling electricity over my skin. As if all the synapses were firing at once. The heat built in my core until I was on the edge of eruption. The tingle started in the base of my spine, and I leaned into it. Leaned into every sensation, every touch, every lick.

I slid my hands into his hair, scoring his scalp with my fingernails. And he shuddered, just before growling low. He tucked a hand under my T-shirt, sliding over my belly, stopping just under the edge of my bra.

Oh, God, yes. Please, God, just let him slide up a little bit more. I wanted his hands on me. I wanted to know if he would be rough, gentle, anything. I was so down for it all. All I wanted was his hands.

Then suddenly, they were gone. Trevor tore his lips from mine. For several long moments, we glared at each other. Well, he glared at me, letting me feel the full force of his anger and confusion. For the most part, I could barely keep my eyes open. All I wanted to do was let them flutter closed, so I could escape to that drugged, sexual euphoria. I wanted to live in that place forever.

But that place came complete with an asshole for a roommate.

Trevor shoved me several inches away from him and

scowled, before doing an about-face and marching off to his room. I expected him to slam the door and braced myself for the loud bang. Instead, there was only a soft but audible click.

6

J esus Christ. What the fuck did I just do?

One second, I'd been giving her shit about her little playmate. The next, my tongue was in her mouth, and she tasted so fucking good I could've come just from that. Another thirty seconds, and I might have had the chance. And I knew she'd been close, too. So close. I was so tempted to go back out there. I wanted to watch her as she came, working her hips over me. God, I wanted her so bad. Shit was way out of hand. At this point, I couldn't tell the difference between my constant fantasies and the reality.

What the hell is wrong with you? I knew what the hell was wrong with me. I had the hots for my sexy roommate.

But fuck, I knew better. She was Professor Washington's

niece. There was no way I could do that. The whole thing was a recipe for disaster. My advisor had the kind of tech contacts that could set me up for life. Jesus, with her contacts, I could get a job at SpaceX if I wanted. And she liked me. She'd already written a couple of great recommendations for internships, but for the jobs I really wanted, those were still pending.

I'd always made it a rule not to shit where I ate. So what was the problem now?

Oh, I knew what the problem was. The little librarian out there was fucking with me. Running around in her cardigans. Every time I saw one, I wanted to rip it off, and use it to tie her to the bedpost. *Lots of girls wear them, asshole.* Well, other girls didn't wear them like Natalie. On her, cardigans were lingerie.

My hands twitched. I'd been so close to cupping her full tits. If I had, I'd have fucked her right there. End of story. Done deal. Because she had the most gorgeous, God-given set of perfect tits I'd ever seen in my life. Or at least it looked that way from a distance. From a distance being the key word. That was the only way I should ever look at her from now on. A distance that had obstacles in between.

I ran my hands through my hair as I paced the length of my

bedroom. I had so fucked that up. How did I come back from that?

Or maybe you don't. Since you've already fucked it up, why not march on back out there, kiss her again, and see where it takes you? The killer of it was, I didn't think about where it would take us. I already knew.

My bed, her bed, the couch. That fucking countertop. Basically any flat surface. Also, the shower. No. No. No. Things were still salvageable. They had to be. We could talk about it: how things had gone too far, and it wouldn't happen again.

Is that really what you want to do? The devil on my shoulder wouldn't shut up.

Shit, I needed advice. Maybe Cage could help. Besides, I could call and check in on my sister at the same time. I dragged my phone out of my pocket and dialed my best friend.

Cage answered on the first ring. "Yo." His voice was low, almost cautious.

"Everything okay?" I asked.

There was a beat of silence. "Yeah, great. Perfect."

"Okay? You sure? You sound funny."

"Nope. I'm good. So what's up?"

"Just figured I'd check in on Talia."

"I, uh, saw her this morning. For, uh, coffee. At a cafe."

What the hell was with Cage, anyway? "Well, okay. Things are cool, right?"

There was another pause on the line. "Absolutely. I'd tell you if they weren't."

"Yeah. Actually, I have another reason for calling."

"Yeah?"

I cleared my throat. "I have a situation."

My friend chuckled. "Oh boy, who'd you fuck that you shouldn't have?"

"Shit. Nobody. Yet..." With a deep breath, I told Cage what happened. When I was done, my friend was silent for a moment.

"Let me get this straight. Your advisor, who you're counting on to get you the dream gig of a lifetime, sends her niece to live with you."

"Yeah."

"She must not know my boy." Cage laughed. "Seriously though, is she hot?"

"Yeah. Really hot."

Case chuckled. "And you kissed her?"

"Yeah. I kissed her." I squeezed my eyes shut, trying to exorcise the memory of how soft her lips were from my memory.

"Any chance it was just one of those 'I-meant-to-kiss-your-cheek-but-oops-there's-my-tongue' kind of kisses?"

I had to laugh. "No, man. It just sort of happened. You know, I barely even like her."

Cage sighed. "Look. That's good that you don't like her. That means that you won't let it happen again."

What? "I was pretty sure you would tell me to go out there and bang her senseless."

"Well, if she were any other chick, then yeah. One that wasn't related to your advisor; the one that holds your future by the balls. If that wasn't the case, man, I'd say you go out there and *make* that chick yours. Maybe that would make you less uptight."

I frowned. "I'm not uptight."

Cage laughed. "Man, when was the last time you relaxed, or let yourself lose control of anything?"

"That is not the point." Cage may or may not have a point there. Growing up, I'd been the one who always had shit together. I always volunteered to take care of everyone else. Who knew where I got that from. My parents never put any extra pressure or me or anything, but still, I always felt like I had to push himself.

"Yeah, whatever. My advice?"

"Yeah, that's why I called your stupid ass."

"Look, I suggest you get laid. You find someone else. Someone very, very hot. Use that pretty face of yours. Chicks have never been a problem for you. You just have all these things called standards. But now, no more standards. You will bang the hottest girl you can find. Because you *cannot* fuck the woman who is living in your apartment. You hear me?"

I frowned. "Yeah, I feel you. I'm not fucking her." And I wasn't. But that didn't mean I wasn't going to think about it. It looked like I was going to be spending a lot of time in the shower.

"And while we're having this conversation, you may not want

to think about her, you know, when you're letting off some steam."

Fuck. "What do you mean?" I swallowed hard.

"I mean, it's going to be a lot harder to get her out of your head if you keep thinking about her naked. So, whatever extracurriculars you've got going on, which I don't want to know about, thank you very much, I would stop them. Right the fuck now."

"I don't know what you're talking about. The thought never crossed my mind," I lied.

"Yeah, sure, whatever you say."

I was eager to change the direction of the conversation. "So, what's going on with you? Anything new?"

For a moment it sounded like Cage was choking. "Actually man, I gotta go. I have class in ten minutes, so I'll call you later and we'll catch up?"

"Yeah, sure. Just call me later." I hung up with my friend and dropped back on my bed. This was going to be next to impossible. But I could do it. I had to.

———

I STARED at the piece of paper on the front of the refrigerator and seriously contemplated burning it. A chore list? Trevor had kissed me and practically incinerated my panties. Then he had the nerve to avoid me and post a chore list?

I grabbed the paper and scowled as I read it again. Not only had he listed all the cleaning tasks that needed to be done, as if I wasn't capable of cleaning up after myself without his help, but he'd actually drawn up a schedule of when we could each use the living room! What the hell? Now I wasn't even allowed to use the living room when he was in there?

I threw the list on the counter and pulled a mug down from the cabinet.

I wonder if Trevor will fine me for using his favorite coffee mug, I thought bitterly. Seriously, what the hell was his problem? I was a good roommate. I even cooked and shared food with him.

The kiss had been a mistake, obviously. But it didn't mean he needed to treat me like I had some contagious disease. If he didn't want to be around me, that was fine with me. But he didn't need to treat me like some prisoner or an unwanted houseguest. I was paying rent, damn it. Apparently, he thought he was so irresistible that I wouldn't be able to keep my hands off him if we were in the same space.

I looked down at the mug in my hands, and then quickly put it back. No, I wasn't going to take this sitting down. If this was going to work, Trevor needed to learn that I wasn't some pushover he could dictate to.

And I knew just how to make him pay. I was heading to the bar. And he wouldn't know what hit him. So what if I changed into skintight jeans and a low cut top before going out? If Trevor drooled over what he could never touch again, even better. The jerk deserved to have blue balls after treating me like I'd forced that kiss. He'd been just as into it as I was at the time, maybe even more. Unless I'd imagined his hands roaming all over my ass.

I didn't bother moving my car, but instead just walked the three blocks, thankful I'd put on my boots with the chunky heel.

When I walked in, I saw a few familiar faces. It was more crowded now than when I'd first come. People actually did this every night? I couldn't imagine spending my leisure time hanging out in some douche bar hoping to land a rich guy. Maybe that was judgmental, but I couldn't help thinking that it made total sense that Trevor worked here. He was probably used to desperate women who'd do anything for a guy with a fat wallet.

Well, he had better get used to dealing with women like me, the kind who didn't take any bullshit.

Once I finally pushed past a giggly crowd of women standing around a guy in a suit, I got to the bar. I scanned behind the bar, but there was only the guy from the other night.

What if he wasn't even here? I'd assumed that he was going to work when he left, but he could have been going somewhere else. My anger had probably just forced me to walk over here for nothing.

Then Trevor came out of the back.

Immediately, his eyes locked on me. His face hardened, and he tapped the guy behind the bar on the shoulder to whisper something. He nodded and then walked over to me.

"What can I get for you?"

I fumed as Trevor turned his back to me. So he'd decided to ignore me? Whatever, two could play that game. He might refuse to talk to me, but he couldn't make me leave if I was a paying customer. I was willing to bet that he'd get tired of seeing me sitting there eventually.

"I'll have one of those watermelon drinks, please. The Ladies' Orgasm. Thanks."

The guy barked out a laugh, then started making my drink, but he paused often to glance over at Trevor. I wondered what Trevor had told him. Definitely not the truth: that his roommate was there to chew his ass out for being a presumptuous prick.

"Here you go, darlin'. Enjoy."

"Thanks." I slid the drink closer and took a long sip. Immediately, my head started swimming, and I coughed.

Damn, this drink was strong. Now I really wanted to know what Trevor had told the guy. Maybe to make my drinks so strong that I'd end up comatose? I wouldn't put it past him.

I looked up to see Trevor watching me with a little smile on his face. I smiled back. He thought he'd won, but I knew something he didn't.

I liked my drinks strong.

I took several more long sips, and then raised my hand to catch the other bartender's attention. When he approached, he looked shocked to see my drink was almost gone.

I grinned. "Another one, please."

7

___

She was stubborn, I would give her that.

I stole another glance at Natalie, who was now working on her third drink. This time, the real Dick Lick. I grimaced. I'd asked Martin to work that side of the bar for me, knowing that he tended to make drinks strong. Natalie was a lightweight. I'd figured she'd have one drink, maybe two, and then tap out.

But no. Natalie looked like she was just getting started. I groaned. I'd have to make sure she got home okay. Even though I didn't want to talk to her, there was no way I'd let her leave alone after having that many drinks.

That was probably what she'd been counting on.

And I was closing, so I couldn't even claim the need to leave early.

Martin approached, wiping his hands absently on the towel tucked into his waistband. "Your girl has some staying power. Even I'm impressed."

I scowled. "She's not my girl."

Martin just raised an eyebrow. "Oh, sorry. I just assumed she was an ex or something."

"No. She's my roommate."

"And you wouldn't even talk to her. That's fucked up." Martin chuckled as he walked away.

It *was* pretty fucked up, I had to admit. I could even admit that it wasn't fair to blame Natalie for the fact that I found her so tempting. But the only other alternative was to blame my dick.

As the next two hours passed, I watched as Natalie drank and chatted with the man sitting next to her. I clenched my fists around the glass in my hand.

The dude was leaning so close that he was in danger of falling into Natalie's cleavage, all of which was currently on display in the low cut shirt she was wearing.

I groaned. How was I supposed to avoid thinking about her when she had those luscious tits propped up like ripe fruit? Sweat broke out on my forehead when the guy stood up and whispered something to Natalie.

What if she tried to leave with him? I couldn't let her go home with some asshole while she was drunk, no matter how mad I was at her. I put the glass I'd been wiping down behind the bar, ready to go over and intervene if necessary. Luckily, Natalie shook her head and the guy left with one last, longing glance in her direction.

Yeah, I know, buddy, keep dreaming.

"Okay, I'm out of here. My dogs are killing me." Martin patted me on the shoulder as he left.

That was when I realized it was almost closing time. Natalie waved gaily at Martin as he left, as if they were long lost friends. I chuckled. Considering how many drinks she'd had, they probably were friends by now. I was sure I was going to pay for this tomorrow. Once Natalie sobered up, she'd no doubt give me hell for ignoring her all night.

But first, I had to figure out how to get her home.

After cleaning up and locking up in the back, I grabbed my coat and came back up front. Natalie was leaning on the bar heavily, her head propped on her arm. I approached, and she watched me warily.

"Oh, now he comes over to talk to me. This is just great," she mumbled. Her words slurred slightly. I was impressed that she was still sitting upright.

"It's time to go. We need to catch a cab."

"I walked here," Natalie spat.

I rolled my eyes. Just my luck that she'd be feisty even when she was drunk.

"Maybe so, but I bet you can't walk all the way home now. Come on."

"No. I came here because I have something to say. I'm going to say it!" She slipped slightly and had to catch herself by slapping a hand on the bar top.

Ignoring her protests, I looped one of her arms around my neck. I was prepared for her to hit me, or fight it, but instead she buried her face in the crook of my neck with a little grumble. She nuzzled around for a while, before grabbing the front of my shirt and pulling me closer.

"Why do you have to smell so good?"

She sounded angry about it, but her hand kept moving over

my chest. I ignored the tingles of sensation shooting from my chest down to my groin. I bit my cheek when her hand traveled a little lower and rested on my belt buckle.

"What are you doing?" I managed to get out between gritted teeth. If her hand went any lower, she'd have a handful of something very hard.

"This," she whispered. Then Natalie tugged me down until our lips met in a fierce kiss. I groaned into her mouth, instantly forgetting my resolve to stay away from her, just enjoying the sensation of her hot little mouth sucking on mine. I couldn't help myself.

Jesus, she was perfect. Natalie pressed her chest against me and made a whimpering sound that shot my desire through the roof. All I could think about was what it would be like to hear that helpless little sound when she was spread out naked in my bed, while I buried my cock in her pussy.

It wasn't until she tried to slide her hands up and under my polo shirt that rationality returned. *Hands off. Hands off*, I thought. I dragged my lips off of hers and took a deliberate step away from her. Okay, make that two steps.

"We're not going to do this. Not like this. You're drunk."

"I am not. Just say you don't want me."

I swallowed hard. "You know that's not true. If we do this, you're going to be stone-cold sober. You will remember everything about it. Tonight is not that night."

She kissed my neck.

"Wait, Natalie. Come on." I managed to separate from her lips, but her hands were still roaming all over my chest. "We have to go home."

It took a lot of maneuvering to get her out of the bar, lock up, and then flag down a cab. Once we were inside, Natalie tried to climb in my lap. I closed my eyes in frustration. I must have done something terrible in a former life to deserve this, being groped by the one woman I'd decided was off limits. Finally, I allowed her to sprawl halfway over me while kissing my neck. It was only three blocks, but it felt like the slowest cab ride ever. I gave the first two bills in my wallet to the driver, hoping I hadn't overpaid, all while trying to separate Natalie from my neck.

"Come on, honey, we're home."

At my words, the disgusted look on the cab driver's face softened a little. I wasn't sure why I cared, but I didn't like the idea that someone thought I was an asshole, about to take advantage of some drunk woman.

Natalie, however, thought my words were funny. "Honey! I'm your honey? You don't even like me."

Luckily, the driver couldn't hear that part, since we were already out of the cab. I finally gave up on getting Natalie to walk and just scooped her up. She grabbed onto my neck so hard I almost choked.

"Don't drop me! I'm scared of heights!"

I laughed as I carried her up the stairs. Luck was on my side, finally, since there was only one other person in the lobby. Natalie continued to mumble random things as I carried her down the hall to our apartment. I set her on her feet briefly so I could open the door, and then picked her up again.

When I got to her room, I pushed open the door, and placed her carefully on the bed. She blinked up at me sleepily, as I helped her get her arms out of the jacket she was wearing. It was too light for the weather, but I guessed she probably wasn't ready for just how cold the fall season was in Boston. It made me wonder about her life before she came here. Where was she from? Why had she needed a place to live so suddenly? All the questions swirled around my brain as I looked down at her.

She'd curled up on her pillow, her boots still on. I said, "Do me a favor. Hold on to the headboard."

She did as I told her, and I helped her pull off her boots and jeans. She took off her own top. When she went for her bra, I had to stop her. "Oh no, you don't."

"Why don't you want me?" she whispered.

I swallowed. If she only knew. "Go to sleep."

Blinking sleepily, she finally mumbled, "Please stay."

I couldn't help himself. "Just until you fall asleep."

Letting the exhaustion take hold, I was left wondering just who was the beautiful stranger living in my apartment.

8

What the hell was a piece of sandpaper doing in my mouth?

I tried to peel my lips apart and move my tongue back and forth, but all I got was that scratchy *shht, shht* sound. Gross. What the hell had crawled into my mouth and died?

I rolled over, and immediately regretted that action, as an elephant delivered a swift kick to my skull. What did I do to deserve this special brand of hell?

Even as I rolled over, it felt like I had to grapple with a thousand orangutans just to get my body to move the way I wanted it to. That was it, I was never drinking again. *Ever.* Like never, ever.

I felt like dirt. Worse than dirt. I felt like the sludgy slime I sometimes saw on the streets after it rained. Yeah, that's what I felt like.

Just what the hell had I been drinking last night?

Last night...

Oh, no. No. No. No.

I tried to lift my head as a memory tickled the back of my skull, forcing my to recall, *teasing* me with hints and images of Trevor. His lips. His cocky smile. His hands. His tongue...

Screw the elephants. I snapped my head up. With that jerky movement, I immediately clutched my skull. But I forced my eyes open as I clung on to the sliver of that memory.

The bar. We'd been at the bar. I forced my brain to concentrate, even though it clearly didn't want to. The other bartender, what was his name? Martin? He'd been mixing my drinks. *Real* drinks. Drinks that had copious amounts of alcohol. So much alcohol.

He'd made all the proper versions of the drinks Trevor had made me the first time I'd visited the bar. They also tasted good, but I could tell there was definitely alcohol in them.

And this time, I was paying the alcoholic Irish piper.

I'd been so drunk. Okay maybe not *that* drunk, but definitely way more than tipsy.

The memory of Trevor's lips on mine assailed me. Oh, hell, I'd kissed him? I closed my eyes and tried to focus.

We'd been in the bar after closing, and... what happened? What did I say? The words eluded me. But the actions, those were clear as crystal.

He'd been trying to take me out of the bar. I'd looped my arms around his neck, and then, kneeling on the barstool, I'd laid one on him.

God, even now, the pleasure slammed right into me, chasing up my spine. The lust washed over me as the memory became more vivid. I remembered his tongue, his hands, his low growl as he'd kissed me and licked into my mouth. While he'd slid his lips over mine, his hands had stayed at my hips, grasping tight, as if he was barely leashing the hunger.

Slowly, the bits and pieces filtered in, and the memory clarified. I'd tried to slide my hands up under his polo shirt, and he'd dragged his lips from mine, stepping back and away from me.

His words had been spoken through clenched teeth. "We're not going to do this. Not like this. You're drunk."

Oh, God, my stomach lurched. Did I have to throw up? Or was the sudden onset of nausea from Trevor's stinging rejection?

After a few deep breaths, the nausea passed, and I remembered him putting me in a cab for the short ride home.

Despite his words, I'd had my hands all over him, trying to convince him that he wanted me.

Each time I'd tried to slide my hands over his body, he'd just kept my hands gently clasped in his, and eventually picked me up into his arms, and carried me into my bedroom.

What the hell is wrong with you? First you make the mistake of picking a guy like Brian. Then you throw yourself at your roommate?

I needed help. Surely, I had some kind of personality disorder. *Or maybe you're just a glutton for punishment.*

I glanced at my body, dragging the sheet away from me, and noted that I was in my bra and panties. I'd definitely gotten out of my clothes last night. Had Trevor helped?

Just the thought of it made prickly heat spread all over my skin.

Jesus. I had to apologize, and eating that much crow was going to be seriously unappetizing. But I had to do it.

Because there was no excuse for last night. I'd gotten way too drunk, and tried to use that as an opportunity to go after something I wanted. Because I'd lost my damn mind, and thought it would be a really good idea to get rid of my sexual frustration with my roommate.

I heard the shower turn on next door. Great. So he was awake. Well, I might as well get up and put the coffee on. At least I could be caffeinated when I had to eat my morning crow.

When I pushed to my feet, I heard the moaning from the bathroom. As usual, when I heard him getting his morning workout on, my whole body throbbed just thinking about him.

Thinking about all those wet muscles in the shower had my hot center pulsing, throbbing, making me want to feel him inside me.

Jesus Christ, thinking about what he was doing in there was not going to help the —

"*Natalie.*"

Holy shit, did he just say —?

Despite what common sense told me to do, despite what my brain cautioned against, I tiptoed closer to the wall to listen. That's when I heard more moaning and more talking...

"Yeah, that's it. Jesus, Natalie...*fuck*..." He growled, then let out a long, low moan.

Holy shit. All this time, Trevor had been masturbating to *me*.

———

I HUMMED as I served up breakfast.

I couldn't explain it, but I was in a hell of a good mood. Last night with Natalie had been...intense. But I had a new way of looking at it now. It had been one of those fluke things. *Yeah, right.* Any second now, she was going to come out of the bedroom, and things would go right back to normal.

I'd gotten really good at lying to myself lately.

The truth was, there was a part of me that wanted to say, "Fuck the consequences". I'd kissed her twice now. And both times, I'd felt like someone pretty much lit me on fire. She was an itch I couldn't scratch, no matter how many times I went back for more.

More than that, she was cute. Like, really cute. And funny. Maybe the two of us could work something out like adults.

Like fuck buddies.

No. My dick twitched as if to say, *hell, yes.*

Shit, I didn't know. I rubbed my eyes. I didn't know anything right now.

She opened her door and shuffled out in her pajamas. Oh, so she'd gotten dressed along the way. Because last I saw her at about five this morning, she was in her bra and panties. Lush curves spilling over the top of flimsy lace.

No. Not going there. I wasn't going to remember a damn thing about the softness of her skin as I'd held her until she went to sleep. Or the little contented sighs she made when she was dreaming. Or the way her bow-shaped lips parted as she slept. *Nope.* I was just going to continue making breakfast and keep my hands busy, so maybe I wouldn't lose my control and screw her on the nearest flat surface.

"Morning. I made breakfast. Nothing like a big breakfast to help soak up all that alcohol."

She jumped when I spoke, and I frowned. Maybe she was embarrassed about what happened last night?

"You made me breakfast?"

I shrugged. "Well, I needed to eat. And I figured you probably weren't feeling so hot this morning, so I made extra. It's no big deal."

She still had yet to meet my gaze when she joined me at the kitchen island and dragged out a stool. Okay, so we were going to have to talk about it.

I dragged in a steadying breath. "About last night. It's not a big deal, okay? How about we both just forget it happened, and how drunk you were. Okay? Like a reboot."

Her gaze flickered to mine, and then skittered away again. "Yep, got it. Reboot. Done."

She still wouldn't look at me.

It bugged me, and part of me wanted to make her meet my eyes. But maybe the two of us had been sniping at each other for too long. It's not like she knew she was starring in my fantasies and giving me an epic case of blue balls. That was on me. I was the one who needed to get my shit together. So I extended an olive branch.

"I'm off today. I figured you and I haven't actually gotten a chance to know each other yet properly. So what better way than with a bad action movie marathon? How do you feel about a little *Cyborg*?"

This time, she did meet my gaze. And then she turned bright pink. "Okay. I do need to go to the library later, though. I'm supposed to meet Alex for a study session."

"Okay, what time?"

She shook her head. "Not until four."

I didn't know why, but I was really happy she didn't have to go until later this afternoon. "That's hours away. Prepare yourself for some classic bad action lines."

Her gaze skittered back to her plate. "Thank you for breakfast. My stomach was threatening to revolt. I'll grab a shower after the first movie."

"Sounds like the perfect plan. A lazy day getting to know my roomie." I tried to sound chipper. Fuck, I had to try. Maybe if we were friends, I wouldn't be so damned obsessed with her. *Yeah, good luck with that.*

We worked in companionable silence cleaning up after breakfast. Despite myself, I liked having her as a roommate. After Courtney, I'd thought I'd hate having someone else around. But it wasn't bad. My extracurricular shower activities notwithstanding, obviously.

She was considerate, neat, and for the most part I didn't notice she was there, really. Except for the candles. They made the place smell nice. *Like her.* And she could cook. She always labeled things with notes like, "I made extra, help yourself."

And you've been a twat to her.

Yeah, I had been. But that was going to change now.

When we settled in for the movie, she parked it on the couch as far away from me as humanly possible, and curled herself up into a tight little ball.

It wasn't like I could blame her, though. Twice now, I'd practically mauled her. *More like you practically mauled each other.* Just thinking about it had my dick standing at attention.

I was suddenly glad I'd already changed into jeans after my shower. That shit would be impossible to hide in sweatpants.

We'd figure this out eventually. The two of us could settle in. We needed to. We were grown-ups, after all. *Barely.* But it couldn't be that hard. We were both smart, knew what we wanted, and while we'd slipped and made out a couple of times, that wasn't going to define us.

The two of us could get along *and* keep our hands to ourselves. We could hang out, be friendly, even. Watching movies like this was fine.

I slid my gaze over her and noticed how long the column of her throat was. So delicate. I wanted to kiss that spot just behind her ear.

Fuck. I snapped my gaze forward, forcing it back to the television. What the hell was wrong with me? All during breakfast, I'd had to battle myself not to stare at her tits. She wasn't wearing a bra, so that was one hell of a herculean effort.

She had her robe mostly pulled around her, but with every move and jostle, my peripheral vision had noted the bounce, and it made me salivate. Did she like her nipples licked? Did she like a gentle touch? A firm one? *Jesus Christ*, just thinking about pinching her nipples had me clearing my throat and adjusting my jeans.

I let another gaze wander over, trying to ascertain if she had any idea of the direction of my thoughts, but she wasn't even paying attention to me. Instead, she was mouthing the words that Van Damme spoke on the screen.

I blinked. "Seriously, you know all the words?"

Natalie grinned. "Yeah. Is that bad?"

I chuckled, even as I shook my head. "Nope. Not at all. But one would think you would save the memorization of lines for movies that deserve it. You know, more highbrow action movies, like Rocky."

"Oh, I do. I know all the words to Rambo, too."

Was she for real? Because I might be a bit in love with her. She was the perfect girl rolled into one. Hot as fuck, smart, had that nerdy thing going for her, and she also liked action movies. Come on. It was like my own personal walking, talking wet dream.

If she told me she knew how to code in C++ as well, I might come right now. Just like that. Just from that knowledge alone.

After we finished the first movie, we switched to Segal. Several times one or both of us would grab a snack, a drink, use the bathroom. But we always returned to the couch, sitting closer and closer than before, eventually sharing a blanket. I liked being this close to her. She smelled so goddamned good. Strawberries and something else.

It was driving me fucking insane. To wake up to that smell had been pure torture on my dick. Which was why I'd already taken care of that little problem once this morning.

Okay, fine. *Twice*, if I was being honest.

After I'd left her room at five o'clock, I'd tried to go back to my own bed. Problem was, all I could smell all over my body was Natalie. The strawberries. All I could feel was her skin, her hair. So I'd taken hold of my dick and tried to cure the problem.

Never mind that I'd told Cage that I wouldn't anymore. That I'd find someone else to screw. I didn't *want* to screw anyone else. I wanted to screw Natalie.

But you can't.

Yeah, well, I'd tried telling my dick that. Fucker was in no mood to listen. But if we were friends, maybe this insane, torturous need would stop. Maybe once I saw her as a real person, I would stop thinking about all the different ways to fuck her.

Like right now, I could drag her under me, tug the pajama bottoms down, unzip my jeans, and fuck her on the couch. Or even better, she could climb on top of my lap. That fantasy had been long-running. And that way her tits would bounce in my face. Or I could bend her over the back of the couch and slide my dick in her—*No. Stop it.*

Jesus Christ. I was going insane. If I kept this up, I would need another fucking shower. And seriously, that shit was getting out of hand. Even I knew I had a problem now.

Question was, what the fuck was I going to do about it? *Because you still can't fuck her.* There would be no fucking winning with this one. Especially not since she was my advisor's niece. And especially not since I liked her. *Too much.*

At the end of the movie, she stretched her arms overhead, arching her back, pretty much putting her tits on display. I couldn't help it. Shit, I tried. I really, really did. But my gaze wandered over and landed directly on the most perfect pair of breasts I'd ever seen.

And, holy fuck, her nipples were hard. I couldn't help it. I licked my lips, wondering if she was cold, or if it was something else. Like maybe she was feeling the tension between us and wanted me too?

Yeah, I was a douchebag. I knew it. And for the first time, I was a little ashamed by it. I didn't want to be having these constant thoughts about her. Fuck, I wasn't used to being like this with any girl.

Usually when I wanted someone, that shit was easy. Smile, flirt, next thing I knew, some girl was handing me her panties and bending over, climbing on top of me, or sucking my dick. It was all pretty easy. And then I'd gotten into a relationship and had my heart torn out. Yeah, I wasn't exactly eager to repeat that experience.

Natalie was different. But I'd thought that about Courtney, too.

I shoved the thought aside when she pushed herself to her feet. "I'm going to take a shower. I've spent far too long in my pajamas."

I grinned at her. "But they're so cute, though. Kittens look good on you."

She flushed and rolled her eyes, heading straight for her bedroom.

It would really be best if I did not think about her naked and soaped up in the shower. But as the water turned on, that's exactly how I imagined her.

Because you're a dick.

Yes. I was. And I was now a tortured dick, so life was a bitch.

For some reason, though, her shower stopped. She came back out in a robe holding her shower stuff. "I'm getting nothing but cold water. Do you mind if I—if—maybe I could —use your shower again?"

"Yeah. Of course."

She flushed and didn't meet my gaze as she shuffled past me to my bedroom.

What was wrong with her? I frowned at her as she hustled into my bedroom. And then a thought slithered into my mind.

Oh, shit. Had she—? No.

There was no way she could hear me. When I heard the water in the shower turn on, I double checked to make sure that she wasn't coming out, and went into her bedroom. As I drew closer to the bed, my stomach plummeted.

Oh, I could hear the shower, all right. I could also hear her humming to herself.

I could hear *everything*.

Which meant she'd heard *everything*.

Everything I'd done from the moment she moved in, she'd heard it all if she'd been in her bedroom.

My skin burned. She'd definitely been in her bedroom this morning when I took a shower. So she'd heard me calling her name. Heard me telling the imaginary Natalie to suck my dick.

Fuck!

This was so bad. She'd known all along. Known I wanted her. Frantically, my mind searched my memory banks. That was probably the reason she couldn't look me in the eye.

I headed back to the living room, and ran for the couch when I heard the water turn off. Plopping onto it just as she came out, her hair wet, robe tied tightly around her waist.

"You were able to find some hot water?"

She nodded "Yeah, thanks for that. Do I need to call the super?"

I shook my head. "You get ready to go to the library. I'll give him a call."

"Thank you. I appreciate it." Again her gaze skittered away from mine.

She was dressed in a skirt and T-shirt with her Converse on and had her hair in her classic ponytail in less than ten minutes. "Well, I'll see you later. Thanks for today. Breakfast and everything. It was exactly what I needed. And thanks for forgetting all about, you know, last night."

Yeah, forgetting about it. The hell I was. "Yeah, of course. Have a good study session."

She licked her lips, and she didn't look like she wanted to go anywhere.

"Is there something else you needed?"

She shifted on her feet. "You're sure that nothing else happened last night? My memory is still foggy. I didn't do anything, did I?"

I was unsure what she was talking about, but I wanted to assuage her fears. "Nothing happened."

She nodded. "Okay. I'll see you later."

I watched her walk out. I wanted her. She wanted me, too. Maybe forgetting about last night was the last thing we needed to do.

She'd been listening to me all this time, and last night, she'd made a move. Maybe it was time to pay her a little visit at the library.

9
———

It wasn't exactly like I was running away. But the library felt like a retreat. Trevor had been really sweet today, considering everything that happened the previous night. But if I'd been confined with him for another minute, I was going to lose my damned mind.

Through the series of three movies, all I could think about was the way he'd said my name in the shower. How could I be expected to hang out with him after that? As if everything was cool. Like nothing had happened.

So of course, instead of concentrating, I'd kept thinking about all the ways he could touch me. At one point, it had made my nipples hard. Trevor Hamilton was walking, talking, breathing sex appeal, and I was only so strong.

But add in the sweet stuff too, and I was going to fold like a house of cards and beg him to screw me silly. For the love of God, the man had fed me. *So what? You feed him all the time.* I shoved aside the rational part of my brain. It did make sense, if I was cooking, to make extra. But this was different. He'd *deliberately* cooked for me. To help me feel better.

My phone chimed and I lunged for it, a part of me thinking that it might be Trevor, asking me what I wanted for dinner.

No, idiot, he is not your boyfriend. This is not how these things happen.

The shitty thing was, I wasn't looking for a boyfriend. After Brian, all I wanted to do was focus on school, and break out of my shell a little. A boyfriend wasn't part of the bargain. And doing things on my own terms would be hard with a boyfriend. Not to mention, Trevor was just like Brian.

He had the smarts, and he beat Brian by miles in the looks department. Someone that hot would burn me eventually. And finding another apartment in the city would be next to impossible. So no screwing my roommate. It was a simple rule...but why was I finding it so hard to stick to?

I swallowed disappointment that the text wasn't from Trevor. It was Alex, telling me he was running late.

I sighed and was glad I'd brought other coursework along. I managed to work for another thirty minutes before my phone chimed again. This time it was Trevor. Just seeing his name come up on the screen had my heart doing a flippy thing. I had it bad.

Trevor: Meet me on the third floor.

I frowned. He was here? Why? I glanced around the library. It wasn't exactly empty, but there weren't many people around. Why did he want to meet me on the third floor? Nobody ever went up there. The upperclassmen liked to freak out the freshmen and tell them it was haunted.

Nevertheless, I grabbed my phone and headed to the third floor. The floor was only partially lit, the auxiliary lights coming on the further down the stacks I walked. Quietly, I called out his name. "Trevor?"

There was no answer at first, and the hairs on the back of my neck stood at attention. This was probably the start to some horror movie. He better not be screwing with me, lest I go all Carrie on his ass.

As most of the library was digitized now, the only people who ever came up here were the history majors who needed some obscure text. The emptiness gave it an extra-eerie feeling as my tennis shoes squeaked on the linoleum. "Damn it, Trevor, where are you?"

The lighted distance between the stacks was shorter and shorter now. If I wanted to extend them, all I had to do was press a button, but there was clearly no one down at this end.

Suddenly, he stepped out of one of the darkened stacks. "I'm right here. You don't have to shout."

I clutched my chest as I whirled around. "Jesus Christ, you scared the shit out of me." I hit him, and didn't miss the fact that he was all hard muscle beneath his T-shirt. "What do you want? Why are we meeting up here? You couldn't just call?"

He licked his lips. "Well, when you were leaving earlier, it occurred to me that maybe we had more to talk about."

"Something you couldn't talk to me about downstairs?"

He took my hand and tugged me into the shadows. When he bracketed me against a shelf with both arms, I swallowed hard. Why did he smell so good? It made it impossible to think with him around.

"We could go back downstairs and talk about how you've been hearing everything in the shower. You want me to discuss that around your study buds? You want me talking about how you can hear me, and what I've been saying?

My face went up in proverbial flames. I was probably a lovely shade of lobster right now. "Oh geez, you know?"

"Well, I figured it out after you went to shower in my bathroom and you wouldn't look at me."

I covered my face with my hands. "Oh my God. Do we have to talk about this?"

He worked his jaw. "You've been hearing me every day."

"Not *every* day. Just, you know, the days when you're in the shower and I'm in the room." I shifted my gaze away.

"Why didn't you say anything?"

"You made it clear you didn't like me, and you had zero expectations on us being friends. So what was I supposed to say? 'Hey, I've been hearing you jack off in the shower. Do you need a hand with that?'"

He dropped his head. "Fuck. That might well have killed me. I've been trying for three weeks to keep my hands to myself. And I'm obviously failing. I kissed you in the kitchen that time, and that's only made it worse. It's like getting my hands on you is all I can think about. I thought last night was because you were wasted. But I kinda get the feeling you want me too. Like you were looking for a little liquid courage."

"I–I–I–" What was I supposed to say to that? "I don't remember exactly what happened last night, but I feel like you kept stopping me from doing anything too crazy."

"Yeah. I did. You were wasted. You kissed me. And I kissed you back. I stopped there, though. When I'm with someone, I want them to know they're with me."

"Well, thanks, I guess."

He ran his hand through his hair. "Jesus, Natalie. What kind of guys have you dated where you thank someone for meeting the baseline of decency?"

"You don't want to know."

"Shit, you're right. I don't. Somehow knowing that you could hear me in the shower is like the hottest thing in the world. What I do want to know is if you're climbing walls nearly as badly as I am. Because I can't think of anything else right now. It's difficult to study. I'm fucking distracted at work."

"I'm distracting you?"

He bit his bottom lip and nodded. "Yes. How the fuck can you not know that?"

"I don't know... I just, well look at you. You can have pretty much any woman you want."

"Right now you're the woman who's been occupying my headspace. Your fucking cardigans have been driving me batshit since I met you."

"My cardigans?"

"Yes. Sometimes when you button just the top one, I sit there praying that your tits will pop that last button. I can't seem to get you out of my head."

I shifted on my feet. "So what are we supposed to do about it?"

His hot gaze met mine, and butterflies fluttered somewhere low in my belly.

"I'm fucking tired of fighting."

As he leaned closer, I held my breath. "Trevor, what are you doing?"

"I'm going to kiss you now, Natalie. If you don't want me to, now's the time to say so."

I knew what would happen when he kissed me. I knew that I wouldn't be able to stop. That *we* wouldn't be able to stop. When his lips met mine, we would both be giving in to everything we'd wanted since I moved in with him. But I didn't stop him. Instead, I tipped my chin up.

"Well, if you're going to kiss me, I suggest you make it good."

Trevor smirked. "You might as well hand me your panties now. You won't need them when I'm done with you."

10

———

All I wanted to do was touch her. Just get a small taste before I stopped. *Can you stop? Can you stop what's happening?* The truth was, I didn't know. Because right now, she tasted like heaven.

We were in a public place. This could only go so far. But I'd been on edge for weeks. And I needed just a small taste.

Sliding my hands up the nape of her neck, I gently stroked her cheek as I kissed her. Why did she taste so good? There was a hint of sweetness to her lips that reminded me of the strawberries she always smelled like.

Every stroke of my tongue was met with one of hers, and sent a shiver through me. I growled low, and picked her up to get easier access. Bonus: that little move made her wrap her legs around me. Extra bonus: that also lined my cock up to her sweet center.

When Natalie rolled her hips, she slid right over my rock hard erection, making me groan. With every gasp and moan, she silently pleaded for more. And I wanted to give it to her.

The angel on my shoulder warned me of where we were. *You're in public, you can't do this.*

But the devil was riding me and telling me all the things he wanted to hear. *Just give her one orgasm, then you can walk away. Then you can stop.* In my lust-fogged brain, this sounded like a fantastic idea.

I dragged my lips from hers and kissed along her jaw, then nuzzled her neck. "You smell fucking incredible." Why couldn't I think? I needed to stop this madness, and then I would take her home and bury myself in her for the rest of the night. And probably the next morning.

But the devil won.

When I moved my hand up her thigh, my fingers met the edge of her panties, and they were soaked. *Jesus.* My dick throbbed and I gritted my teeth against the wave of lust. *Take. Taste. Mark.*

I slid my fingers under the elastic of her panties, rolling my thumb over her clit. Her whole body shook and she threw her head back.

With a low, muttered curse she planted one leg on the shelf of the opposite bookcase. She tore her lips from mine and groaned. "Oh my God, Trevor. Yes... right... there."

I watched her face carefully as I rubbed a slow, gentle circle over her clit. Her mouth hung open as she worked her hips into my touch. Jesus, she was beautiful. I wanted more from her. Carefully, I added a finger. Slowly sliding inside her with a gentle retreat. Natalie bit her bottom lip.

"You are so soft," I whispered, adding a second finger. Her eyes popped open and she blinked rapidly, but I didn't gentle the caress. But it wasn't until I curved my fingers and found that bundle of nerves inside, pressing gently, that she broke apart.

I dropped my forehead to hers. "That's it, Natalie. Give it to me." And I stroked her inside over and over again.

"Trevor—Jesus. I'm going..." she bowed her body, and I watched in awe while her pussy clamped around my fingers. *Oh, yeah.* This is what I wanted to see. Natalie open and completely out of control. I fucking loved it. I wanted to make her do it again.

Gently easing my fingers from her, I brought them to my lips. She tasted incredible. "When we get back to the apartment, I want to do this properly. I'm going to make you come with nothing but my tongue."

"I want more." She was far from done with me, and reached for my belt buckle.

I shook my head. "Natalie. You're playing with fire."

"So only you get to tease and torture me? I don't get to do the same to you?"

"You touch my dick, and I'm not waiting until we get home."

"Good." Natalie slid her hands inside my jeans, and I was lost. Her delicate fingers wrapped around me, and then she pumped once. Twice. The third time, my knees buckled.

I choked out, "You think I don't want to come?"

"I want to watch you, too." She flushed. "I've been picturing you in the shower."

Where in the world had she been hiding my whole life? "I love how you think. We need to get home."

"No, we don't. You brought me up here. Are you up for an adventure, Trevor?"

Shit. Was I ever. Between her words, the need I saw in her eyes, and the way her thumb stroked over the tip of my cock and then gently stroked the underside of the tip, I couldn't wait. With shaking hands, I dug in my back pocket for my wallet and fumbled for a condom. When I found it, I tossed the wallet to the ground, and let my jeans fall off my hips slightly.

I had myself sheathed in seconds. All the while, my gaze never left hers. Through clenched teeth I asked, "You sure you want this?"

Natalie nodded. "I need it."

I cupped her ass, lifting her until I nudged her gently, before kissing her again. I guided my cock to her slick, heated core. *Oh, fuck.* If I did this, she would own me. A part of me still rebelled against that, but I didn't give a fuck.

Her eyes widened with surprise, and then she locked onto my gaze again and relaxed.

The second she did that, I sank deep, and we both hissed. *Shit.* My eyes crossed. I was never leaving. She pulsed around me, and I swore I could stay inside Natalie forever.

She dug her nails into my shoulders, and my name was a whisper on her tongue. With each slide and retreat, my knees weakened. Natalie placed her hand above her, using one of the shelves for more leverage as I made love to her.

My gaze occasionally dipped to where we were joined, watching my cock slide in and out of her. When she arched her back, I dipped my head to draw one of her nipples into my mouth.

"Trevor. Yes. Harder. Oh, God. Oh my God."

Against her nipple I muttered. "Quiet, sweetheart, this is a library."

Her response was to tug on my hair, and I couldn't help the soft chuckle. I loved the sounds she made, but this was risky as fuck, and we were going to get caught.

When we were home, I'd focus on her breasts. I had plans for them. I wanted to take my time licking them, kissing them, biting them, fucking them.

When I felt the quiver of her pussy around my dick, I knew she was close. I snapped my hips, and her eyes went wide. To help her along, I worked a hand between us, and found her sensitive clit. My first touch was gentle, but then I stroked more firmly.

"That's it. Come for me. I'm already a little addicted to the sight."

My eyes crossed as her slick walls clamped around my dick and milked me. *Jesus Christ. So tight.* She felt so good. With three more pumps, I was coming apart, as my control fell away.

All that was left of me in the end were the shattered pieces she left. I felt stripped bare as I clutched onto her.

Another orgasm rolled through her, and she tightened around me once more. By that point, all I could do was groan as she rode out the wave.

Holy fuck. I was keeping her. I was definitely keeping her. "You, Natalie, are naughty."

She grinned at me. "That is the first time anyone has ever called me naughty."

I kissed her softly. "Why don't you go get your stuff, and I'll walk you home so we can do this properly?"

"Yeah, I'll just –"

Somewhere down the hall we heard a voice call out, "Nat? Are you in here?"

Her face flushed crimson and she whispered. "Oh my God, Alex. He texted me that he was going to be late."

Fuck him. I eased out of her and helped her quickly readjust her clothes. "Go. Hurry. I'll wait to walk you home."

She hesitated. "Are you sure?"

Hell yeah. I was still half hard. "Yeah, I'm sure. We're sure as shit not done."

"I'm pretty sure my hair looks like I've been freshly fucked."

I grinned. "Good. Besides, you're gorgeous to me. Now go, before your friend finds you with my dick back inside you. Because if you keep looking me like that, I'm going to fuck you again."

Her pupils dilated like she wanted me to do just that. But instead, she scooted out of the shelves and called out, "Alex, I'm down here. I'm headed down."

As her footsteps echoed further away down the hall, I took care of the condom and adjusted my clothes. When I leaned against the stacks, I let my body sag.

Holy fuck. What the hell was I doing?

11
———

I felt like I was floating. It was stupid to feel like everything in my life was instantly brighter and better just because of some hot sex, but there it was. I wasn't too proud to admit that Trevor had rocked my world. My skin was tingling, and I was smiling like a fool.

Nothing could bring me down.

Until we reached the apartment and I saw my Aunt Patty waiting out front. As soon as my aunt turned around, I knew instantly that something was very, very wrong.

"Aunt Patty! What are you doing here?"

Once I got closer, I gasped. My aunt's eyes were red and swollen.

"There you are. I've been calling and calling." Aunt Patty clasped me in a tight hug and I could feel the older woman trembling. "Uncle Sidney is in the hospital. He had a heart attack."

I covered my mouth with my hands. "Oh, no. I'm so sorry, Aunt Patty. My phone was off." I glanced over at Trevor, sure my guilt was written all over my face. My aunt had needed me while I was getting busy with him in the university library.

"I left once they told me they had to do some more tests, just to grab a few clothes. Sidney insisted. You know how he hates for me to hover over him." My aunt twisted her wedding ring around her finger. "I just need to go home quickly."

"Of course, I'll go with you."

Trevor's hand landed on the small of my back, and I was grateful for the connection.

He said, "I'll drive you to pick up your things and then back to the hospital."

Aunt Patty smiled tremulously. "You don't have to do that, Trevor."

"No, I want to. You shouldn't be driving right now when

you're upset."

Somehow, in that cajoling way of his, Trevor managed to convince Aunt Patty to allow me to pack a bag for her, so she could make calls to the rest of our family. I packed several changes of clothes, my aunt's toiletries on the bathroom counter, and a nightgown and slippers. I could only hope I hadn't missed anything vital. My eyes landed on the large pair of slippers next to my aunt's bed. I closed my eyes and prayed that my Uncle Sidney would be all right. I didn't want to think about the alternative.

"Okay, I think I got everything."

"I'm sure it's fine, my dear." My aunt rested a gentle hand over mine. "Thank you for that. And thank you, Trevor, for driving. You were right. I wouldn't have been safe driving alone."

"Anything for you, Professor."

Aunt Patty chuckled. "I think you're safe calling me Patty by now."

Trevor looked in the rearview mirror before pulling away from the curb. "Not a chance. You're still the same intimidating, kick-ass professor I met on my first day of college."

That made my aunt smile, and in that moment I wished I

could lean over the seat and kiss him.

At the hospital, Trevor and I took seats in the waiting room, while my aunt went to check on my uncle's status. About ten minutes later, she came back to lead us to his room. As soon as I saw my uncle sitting up in bed, looking hale and hearty, I burst instantly into tears.

"Now, what's all this? Pat, what have you been telling our girl? Did she think I was dead or something?" Sidney asked.

"Oh, Sidney! Don't talk like that."

My aunt swatted him on the arm playfully, but I could tell that she was just as happy to see him looking so well. The light blue hospital gown did him no favors, and his salt and pepper hair was standing on end in all directions, but he had all the usual spunk of my favorite uncle.

I wiped my face. "I'm just being silly, of course. It just hit me that we hadn't had a chance to have dinner yet."

Sidney smiled in understanding. "Afraid I'd kick the bucket before you had a chance to see me again?" He held open his arms so I could hug him. "Not a chance, little missy. I plan to be around for a long time."

"You'd better be." My aunt's words were soft and heartfelt. She clasped Sidney's hand and kissed him.

I suddenly felt like I was intruding on a very private moment.

"Well, we're going to go and give you guys some privacy. I'm so glad you're okay, Uncle Sidney. Come on, Trevor."

After another hug for both my uncle and my aunt, Trevor and I waved goodbye before walking out into the hallway.

Once we were a few feet away, Trevor let out a heavy sigh. "I'm so glad he's okay. You know, Professor Washington talks about him all the time. I used to think she was a newlywed. Then I found out they've been married thirty years." He shook his head.

"I know. Amazing. That's the real deal, right there."

His eyes locked on mine. "The real deal. I guess you know it when you feel it."

———

I FOLLOWED Natalie out of the hospital, unsure of what to say or do. I wasn't used to being with a girl during such an emotional time. It was telling, actually, to look back and realize how much of my relationship with Courtney had been routine. We'd existed side by side for years, more like fellow travelers than true partners.

At the time, I didn't know just how superficial our connection was, but after watching Natalie with her aunt and uncle, I knew better. I wanted to know everything about her, including the people she cared about. It was a startling feeling, especially since we were just getting to know each other. Such strong feelings had to be because of the intense situation we were in, right? We lived together, and she was my advisor's niece. That was it.

Sure.

"Thank you for driving us today, Trevor. That was really nice of you." Natalie squeezed my arm as we walked through the hospital parking lot toward my car.

The praise made me a little uncomfortable. I didn't like getting kudos for doing the bare minimum of decency. Especially from Natalie. I wanted her to know that she could always expect me to come through for her. Even though we'd had our disagreements, and probably would again, the thought of her not calling me if she was ever in trouble drove me crazy.

"I was happy to do it. I'm just glad your uncle is okay."

Natalie let out a soft sigh. "Me too. I was so afraid that we'd get to the hospital and hear bad news. I can't imagine my

Aunt Patty without Uncle Sidney. They're two pieces of the same puzzle, or at least that's what he always says."

I smiled at the description. "Have you ever felt that way about anyone?"

She broke away to get in the passenger side of the car, and I found myself impatient for her answer. Was there some guy out there holding her heart hostage?

Once inside, I turned to her before I even started the car. "Well?"

She laughed. "I thought I had found that. But what I found was a guy who really liked banging one of his students. Well, a lot of his students, since I wasn't the only one, it turns out."

"Ouch. That sucks. I'm sorry." I really wasn't, because that asshole's bad decisions had brought her to me. If I knew his name, I'd send the guy a thank you card.

"It did suck, but I moved on. I'm here, and I love my classes. What about you? Have you ever felt that way?"

I wasn't sure how to answer the question anymore. So I went for brutal honesty. "My last girlfriend walked out on me after two years together. I was completely blindsided. I loved her. But I guess she didn't feel the same way."

Her sharp intake of breath was comforting.

"Well, it sounds like you're well rid of her. Both of us are well rid of people who didn't appreciate us. I'm done with people wasting my time. I'd rather be alone than led on and then discarded."

"I agree." I glanced over at her, wishing that I wasn't driving, so I could keep my eyes on her face.

"What?" she said after a few minutes. "You keep staring."

"Just watching your eyes get all bright when you're in feisty mode. I like it. That's exactly the kind of attitude that I wish my sister had."

Natalie turned in her seat to face me. "Oh, you have a sister. I didn't know that."

"Her name is Talia. She just transferred to NYU this year. I've been a little worried about her. She's not strong like you are. All Talia has ever cared about are books, and I don't even think she's ever had a boyfriend. I'd hate for her to get taken advantage of."

"You're a good big brother. And I'm sure she's much tougher than you give her credit for. She's related to you, after all. The guy who told me five seconds after meeting that you'd walk around naked if you wanted, and I could shove it."

I winced. "Sorry about that. I can be a bit…"

"Of a dick?" Natalie supplied. "Yeah, I know. I figured that out on my own, thanks."

"Ha, ha. Smartass. You're not exactly an angel yourself. Inviting guys over and talking about cocks in my living room. You knew exactly what you were doing to me."

"Oh? What was I doing to you?" Natalie raised her eyebrows.

"Giving me blue balls, for starters."

She snorted. "That was for our research paper. Not to tease your dirty fantasies."

I parked the car in front of our building. I turned off the ignition and we sat in silence, the only sound in the car my harsh breathing.

"You have no idea how many dirty fantasies I've had about you, Natalie. In my bed, in my shower, hell, even in the kitchen."

"Really?" She looked at me from the corner of her eye. "Want to show me?"

I almost hurt myself, I jumped out of the car so fast. "Upstairs. Right now, you little tease."

12

———

I should have been ashamed. My uncle was in the hospital, and here I was flirting with Trevor like some hussy. But my emotions felt like they'd been caught in a blender, swinging from fear to elation when I discovered that my uncle would be okay. And having Trevor right there by my side the whole time had done something to me.

It was a dangerous fantasy, to imagine that Trevor really cared about me. We were having fun. That was all. I wasn't even ready for something serious after dealing with Brian's bullshit. But I couldn't deny how nice and how arousing it was to have a man take care of things the way Trevor had today. As soon as he'd seen what we needed, he'd taken charge and just done what needed to be done.

A take-charge man was a sexy thing.

Now I wanted to show him just how hot he'd made me.

"Okay, we're upstairs. What should I do now?" I giggled when Trevor almost tripped trying to get his jeans off.

I sat primly on the edge of the couch, watching as he struggled to remove his clothes. When I grabbed the bottom of my shirt, Trevor stopped me with one hand.

"No, let me. I don't want to miss the good stuff."

He focused on the swells of my breasts through my shirt, his hands kneading and shaping. When he tugged, I raised my arms so he could pull the shirt over my head. At his motion, I stood, and allowed him to peel my jeans down my legs. Soon, I stood before him in my bra and panties, shivering under his hot gaze. The way he looked at me made me feel like the sexiest creature on the planet. It was hard to admit, but Brian's betrayal had really shaken my confidence.

Now I had the incredibly hot Trevor Hamilton kneeling at my feet and looking like he was ready to worship me with his tongue. It would be hard for any girl not to get a little buzz from that.

"You are so beautiful, Natalie. I should be taking care of you right now, and yet, you have me thinking about fucking you against the wall."

I shivered at his dirty words. "You are taking care of me. This is what I need."

He regarded me for a long moment before he nodded. "This is what I need, too."

There was something grave about the way he said it, like the words had more meaning than what was on the surface. He unhooked my bra and helped me step out of my panties, his fingers trailing over my skin like I was the most delicate treasure. But before I could examine that too closely, Trevor picked me up and slung me over his shoulder. I squealed in outrage, but secretly was thrilled at the barbaric display.

When he put me down gently on his bed, I spread out my arms, getting comfortable. Our first time hadn't been anywhere near a bed. I flushed and giggled at the thought

"What are you laughing at, beautiful?"

"This is the first time we'll be in a proper bed."

Trevor tilted his head to the side as he thought about it, a gesture I found endearing. Then he shrugged.

"So it is. But it won't be the last. Get used to being in my bed." His mouth covered mine and his tongue pushed past the barrier of my lips.

I could only hold on, digging my fingers into his shoulders as I surrendered to his kiss. He tasted of sweets and coffee, a combination that would always make me think of Trevor. His hand snuck underneath and grasped the curve of my bottom. I gasped into his mouth at the contact, the sudden grip on my flesh forcing my hips to tilt. The new angle allowed him to settle right against my core, making me cry out in delight.

Trevor's dark chuckle only made me wetter. He was so arrogant, but in the bedroom, that wasn't a bad thing. He was arrogant in this case because he knew he had the goods to deliver exactly what I needed. I shivered as he ground his cock against my wet core. I had never been the type to beg, but I knew what he could do with it. And I needed it.

I pushed on his shoulders until he rolled onto his back. A naked Trevor spread out for me to enjoy was an enticing sight. I took the opportunity to run my hands all over his sculpted chest and shredded abs. The man was too beautiful for words. His cock stood up proudly, and I licked my lips when a bead of moisture appeared at the tip.

Trevor groaned. "Fuck, you're such a little tease."

I scooted down on the bed until his cock was right in front of my face, and he could feel the warmth of my breath. He inhaled sharply when I took him all the way to the back of my throat.

"Oh, shit. Natalie, that feels so good."

I moaned around his length, knowing the vibrations would drive him crazy. His jaw clenched, and he let out a strangled grunt. Maybe he was right and I was a tease, because it was incredibly satisfying to watch Trevor unravel as I tormented him with my mouth. He pulsed, thick and needy, on my tongue, and I sucked hard.

"Fuck, yes." Trevor's hand snaked into my hair, and I moaned at the bite of pain. His eyes held mine, and I found myself unable to look away.

It was the most intense connection I'd ever experienced, to allow Trevor to fuck my mouth as he watched the whole thing. I knew it had to be a sexy sight because I felt it, too. He couldn't take his eyes off my mouth, seemingly riveted by the sight of his thick cock forcing its way between my lips.

"Jesus, you are going to kill me." He pulled out reluctantly and I whimpered, not ready to lose that thick, powerful stalk just yet.

But he wasn't done with me, not by a long shot. I moaned helplessly as he didn't release his hold on my hair. I felt completely at his mercy as he turned me around and pushed my head down to the mattress.

"Trevor, please." My pleading only made him chuckle as he got in position behind me. The way he held me down only increased the anticipation since I couldn't see what he was doing; I could only feel.

The first thrust went so deep I cried out in shock. Pleasure bloomed and coiled in my belly as he thrust again, his strong hand still holding me down to take his thrusts. To take whatever he had to give.

I wailed as my orgasm crashed through me, my helpless position only fueling it. Trevor moaned as my muscles tightened around him, riding out my orgasm and stroking deeper to prolong it.

When I collapsed, exhausted, he gave me a few seconds to catch my breath, and then pulled out. When I saw that he was still hard, my eyes flew up to his.

"You didn't–"

He shook his head. "No. I'm not anywhere near done with you."

———

I THRILLED at the sight of Natalie, naked and satisfied in my bed. But something wouldn't let me end this. I needed more than for her to just be satisfied. Something dark inside wanted to hear her scream my name. I needed to take her hard and make sure that I gave her more than any other man ever had.

Why I needed that, well, I wasn't quite ready to examine that yet.

Natalie watched me with glittering eyes as I reached over to the night table and pulled out a strip of condoms. Her breathing got faster as her eyes went down to where I rolled one over my swollen cock. I came down on top of her, using one arm to hold myself up while the other plumped and played with one tempting breast. Her soft moans urged me to taste one sweet cherry nipple, my tongue snaking out to lick it.

Her mouth fell open when she felt my cock slide through her wetness. It felt so damn good that I did it again, using my hard shaft to bump her clit. We moaned together this time, and I lost the tether on my control.

Natalie surged upward at my first deep thrust.

"Trevor! Oh my God." Her nails dug into my forearms as she came again, her internal muscles going crazy around me.

I grunted through the pain, but it only enhanced the visceral pleasure of watching her come. Her orgasm only enflamed me, and I pulled back and slammed home again. Natalie held on as I thrust again and again, keeping pace with me and squeezing me until I thought I'd die from the sheer, white-hot pleasure.

Then she clamped down on me again and I came violently, the convulsive release taking everything I had. All the emotion, all the pain, all the rage came with it, and I felt like I was pouring out my soul. Unable to help myself, I collapsed on top of her, my head pillowed on her full breast.

Once I finally recovered enough to move, I turned my head slowly. Natalie smiled down at me lazily.

"Hi," she said sweetly.

It was such a simple thing, but I knew then that I never wanted to let this woman go.

"Hi," I answered back, happier than I'd been in ages.

Afraid that she'd be able to see how sappy and completely, ridiculously satisfied I was if I looked at her too long, I pulled out of her gently. I needed a shower. Maybe in the time it took to clean my body, I could get my emotions under control.

No woman should have this kind of power over a man's heart. I'd already learned what happened when you let your guard down and allowed yourself to love someone. They had the power to hurt you. Courtney had shared two years of my life and then walked away like it was nothing.

Already, what I felt for Natalie eclipsed every emotion I'd ever had before. It was so big, this sense of rightness that I felt around her, and it scared the hell out of me. If I felt this much for Natalie already, what would happen when she eventually moved on?

Somehow, I didn't think I'd recover a second time.

"I'm going to take a shower." I kissed her forehead, avoiding her searching gaze.

It made me feel like a bit of an asshole that I was leaving her right after sex, but that was how it was supposed to go, right? Casual sex wasn't supposed to be about cuddling and feelings. So I had to cut off the desires that made me want to crawl back into bed and rest my head on her soft breast again. Maybe a cold shower would shock me back to my senses.

Ten minutes later, I looked down at my hard cock and cursed. The cold water hadn't helped at all, and I was still fighting the urge to go back into the room and climb on top of Natalie again.

She's right there, naked and ready, my mind taunted me. *Go and make her yours.*

I was about to turn the water off when slim arms encircled me from behind. Natalie's breasts pressed against my back, and all the rest of my blood shot to his cock.

"Do you mind if I join you?" She reached around me and turned the water temperature back up.

She didn't comment on why I was taking a cold shower after sex, but just glanced down at my erection. Her eyebrow quirked and she grinned.

"You could have let me take care of this, you know. I don't mind."

Before I could blink, she was on her knees and had that hard, aching part of me between her lips. I gave up on gaining any control over the situation, and allowed my head to fall back against the tile.

If I was going down, I might as well enjoy the ride.

13

I stretched my arms over my head and snuggled deeper under the covers. I was exhausted and sore, and I felt freaking amazing. I patted around the bed for Trevor, but he was gone. Instead, I found a note.

I just went to finish work on a project. If you wake up and miss me, come find me.

I grinned, but the rational part of my brain intruded. *Don't get too comfortable.*

I shoved the thought away. But I had to wonder... what was going to happen now? Grabbing a pillow, I dragged it over my head. Physically, we worked. Like, *really* worked. My skin was still buzzing from the electricity of his touch. But what did this mean? He was still getting over his ex, and I clearly had some trust issues.

It's not like we'd had any conversations about what we were doing here. Everything in the library had happened in a blur of hormones and tongues. And then we'd come home to find everything in crisis. So we had to go.

After the adrenaline spike of my uncle's hospital visit, I'd needed comfort. I giggled, thinking about just how he comforted me. There hadn't been much time for conversation.

I still couldn't believe he'd wanted me to stay with him all last night. I hadn't expected it. I hadn't even asked. As soon as I'd received the news, he'd just said "Let's go."

What in the world had I done to deserve him?

He's not yours.

This was true. It seemed like things worked better when we actually had conversations. Which meant we were going to have to address the whole 'Hey, we're still roommates and we boned' situation. Was this a thing, or was it nothing?

Well, how do you feel about it?

I wanted to do it again. And again, and again. I liked him.

Even when he was being an arrogant ass, he was still kind of snarky and funny. But also, he could have those totally sweet moments. Not to mention, he was smart, like *really* damn smart.

Time to stop procrastinating. I ditched the pillow and pushed up to a sitting position in bed. I was so screwed. I really liked him. One moment, we were sniping at each other, well, more him sniping at me, pushing my buttons. The next, he'd kissed me in the kitchen, and I was being distracted by his morning moaning in the shower.

Then the next thing I knew, we were making love in the stacks at the library. And he was holding my hand in the hospital, telling me it was going to be okay.

After Brian, I hadn't thought I was capable of falling for someone again. Trust was a problem. And with someone as good-looking as Trevor, no doubt he had a million girls following him around. Would I be able to trust him? Would I be constantly worried about him screwing someone else?

You're getting ahead of yourself.

Conversation first. And if he wanted to be friends with benefits, I could be okay with that.

No, you can't.

Okay, fine. No, I couldn't. I knew myself. Eventually, I'd be looking for more, and that was where I would get burned. *That's not you. And that will hurt.* Because there would be others.

I had to stop being a coward and go talk to him. We could have this conversation like adults. Because at the end of the day, letting him go now would be a hell of a lot easier than getting really attached to him and having to let him go later.

I tossed on a T-shirt before padding out into the hallway. But when I opened the door, I froze at the sound of a familiar voice.

"I brought you doughnuts. I figured since you were studying hard, and have a sweet tooth, I'd bring you a little sugar to help keep you going," she cooed.

My stomach squeezed, even as I threw up a little in my mouth. That was Jenny of the big-boob and little-brain fame. Despite myself, I couldn't help but lean in and listen.

"Jenny, you can't be here right now."

She shrugged. "Look, I know it's early. And you've probably got studying or some other sexy thing you do shirtless and with glasses on. But you never called me after the other night. And you know, this girl was starting to get her feelings hurt." She sidled up to him. "I figured I'd give you a chance to make it up to me."

Trevor stepped away from her. "I was meaning to call you."

Jenny grinned and stepped forward again. This time she wrapped her hand around his–

I didn't wait to see what else happened. It was time to go.

I was careful to close my bedroom door with a soft click before leaning against it, sharp, ragged breaths tearing out of my chest.

What the hell was wrong with me? How did this keep happening to me? *This is what you get for sleeping with your roommate.* I had to get the hell out of here. Without over-thinking, I grabbed a duffel bag and threw some clothes in before snatching up my backpack. I was dressed and in the hallway in five minutes.

I tried to bypass Trevor, but he called out. "Natalie? Where are you going?"

Unable to help the sob, I blurted out, "I figured you'd be too busy with Jenny to notice me leaving. Don't worry, I'm out of your hair."

I didn't look back when the door slammed behind me.

I CALLED AFTER HER. "Natalie, wait. It's not what it looks like." She was already gone.

I only hesitated for a moment before sprinting into my room and grabbing my running shoes. I barely had them on before I yanked open the front door to go after her. I stopped short when I found Professor Washington with her hand raised about to knock on the door.

"Professor. What are you doing here? Is everything okay with your husband?"

"Yes. He's fine. He's in recovery and doing well. I just came because Natalie forgot her phone." She held up the phone for me to see.

"Oh. You just missed her. I'm actually headed out after her. She's upset. We had a fight. Actually, not really even a fight."

Damn it. Why was I telling her all of this?

My advisor nodded her head. "Do you mind if I come in for a minute?"

I hesitated, because I knew that with every second that ticked by, Natalie was disappearing somewhere, and it would be more difficult to find her. But my brain was at least functional enough to know that I couldn't exactly say no to my advisor.

"Sure. Come on in."

I stepped aside and let her into the apartment. When she stopped at the kitchen counter, she slid Natalie's phone toward me.

"Listen, I appreciate everything you've done for her. Giving her a place to stay after I sort of twisted your arm. And after yesterday, the support you've given her... it's great." She swallowed and licked her lips.

"But?" I stomach cramped. I didn't like where this conversation was headed.

"But, you and I have been working on getting you international opportunities. You made it extremely clear that you wanted to travel and live abroad. You wanted opportunities that got you away from the US for a while so you could broaden your horizons. And that's what we're focusing on."

I frowned. "Yeah? What does that have to do with anything?"

"It can't have escaped you that after everything she's been through, Natalie needs something stable. If you were sticking around, then I would be over the moon. You're a good kid, smart. One of my best students, and I think you got a raw deal with Courtney. But you're *not* staying. You're leaving. My husband and I practically raised that girl, and I know she would be heartbroken. I can see it in her eyes. You already have the power to break her heart."

I shook my head. "That's not what I'm trying to do." I ran a hand through my hair. "I swear I didn't mean for any of this to happen. I don't even *know* what's happening. But I like her."

Professor Washington put her hand over mine on the counter. "Yes. You like her. But even before Courtney left, you were hyper focused on your career. When you had a girl-friend, you chose school. Which, frankly, is what you should choose at this age. You chose to focus on your work and not focus on her. And when the time comes again, you will choose your job. You will choose to leave Natalie behind. Because it's what you have to do. The thing is, as her aunt, I think Natalie deserves more than that."

"So do I."

"Especially after the last guy she dated, she deserves someone who's going to choose her. She deserves someone who's going to love her. Not just someone who's using her as a stop on the way to something else."

She put up her hand to stop me when I started to speak.

"And I don't mean that you're using her. What I mean is, given everything that you want, given who you are, when push comes to shove, you will not choose her. And that's going to hurt her. It's kinder to let her go now."

After she left, I stared at the door for a long moment. There was still time. I could still run after Natalie. I'd check the library. I'd check with her friend Alex, if I could find him. I could still go after her.

Or was Professor Washington right? To me, Natalie was temporary. I wasn't planning on staying here. And she'd just moved here with her own career goals. Maybe I should let her go. It was better to let go now than later, after all.

Except, why was there a burning hole in the middle of my chest?

14

I kicked a patch of grass next to my foot. I looked up as a child ran by screaming.

Okay, maybe a public garden wasn't the best choice for a quiet place to think about things.

But when I'd run out of the apartment, I hadn't known where to go. When I got to the curb, I'd realized I didn't have my phone, so I couldn't even pull up directions to anywhere. I'd told the cabbie to take me to a park just because it was the first thing that had popped into my mind. Now I was sitting here surrounded by happy families while I was miserable.

Trevor, meanwhile, was probably boning big-boobed Jenny back at our shared apartment.

Ugh. What was wrong with me?

You'd think after my experience with Brian, I'd have learned not to mix business with pleasure. Not that Trevor was business, but he was my roommate. And now that we were fighting, it jeopardized my living arrangements.

Could I really stay there while he brought other girls home? I recoiled at just the thought. No way. I wasn't the catfight type, but I'd seriously wanted to scratch that girl's eyes out. Something about Trevor brought out my territorial instincts, and that was alarming.

I'd been with Brian way longer, and I hadn't felt the urge to fight off any of his other girlfriends. But what did that mean? I had a sinking feeling it meant that I'd fallen harder for Trevor. Once the shock wore off and the hurt set in, I was going to be even worse off over this betrayal. Which was a scary thing.

"You know what? No. I'm not going to let him have this power over me." I kicked the dirt by my foot again, scaring a nearby pigeon into flight.

But I was already on my feet, ready to go back to the apartment and have it out with Trevor. He wasn't going to do this to me. I was tired of allowing other people to manipulate my emotions. If he wanted to have another girl, then I was going to just lay it out for him that I wasn't into that. He couldn't treat me like I was disposable unless I let him.

All fired up, I hailed another cab to go back home.

But when I arrived at the apartment, he wasn't even there.

Deflated, I went through the motions of making lunch, and ate a sandwich standing up in the kitchen. But Trevor didn't come back. I did some laundry and even watched a movie, but by the time I got in bed that night, he still wasn't home. I punched my pillow. He'd probably gone to work.

But when I walked into his room the next morning and saw his perfectly made bed, that was when the tears started. He hadn't even come home last night.

He probably stayed with Jenny.

I bit my lip, looking around the empty apartment and wondering what I should do. I finally found my phone on the counter in the kitchen, plugged into the charger. There were no new messages or texts. My eyes caught on my last text message with Alex.

Hey, you busy?

Nope. What are you doing texting me on a Saturday morning? Shouldn't you be humping that HOT roomie of yours?

I sighed.

My roomie is a slimy jerk. Can I come over?

Yes. I need the deets. Because if you did that hottie and aren't happy, that sounds like a story I need to know.

A half an hour later, I was huddled on Alex's couch in his tiny studio apartment, sipping on a cup of tea while he hung, riveted, on my every word.

"I don't even know why I'm so upset," I finished. "It's not like we were really together. It just felt like something, you know?"

Alex rolled his eyes. "Believe me I know. Try feeling that thing with a guy who then tells you he isn't gay. The universe is cruel and deceitful."

I winced. From that perspective, I couldn't complain too much. Plus, at least I'd gotten to experience the best sex of my life. Although that was partially why this was so hard. How could the best lover I'd ever had be the same one who hurt me so easily? The universe really was cruel.

"You are wise, Alex. So wise. I'm going to stop thinking about him. He's just a blip on my radar. And I'm not going to let his man-whore ways run me out of the apartment, either. I can handle him and his skanks coming over if it means I can stay where the rent is affordable."

Alex took my mug of tea and set it gently on the coffee table. "You don't have to pretend like it's no big deal. This guy hurt you. If I wasn't afraid he'd kick my ass, I'd take him out for you. Maybe this is not what you want to hear, but I don't think you should have walked out and let some bitch move in on your territory."

I rested my head on his shoulder. "That's just it, I don't want you to take him out. I just want him to feel the same way I do. Pathetic, huh?"

Alex stroked my hair. "No. Not pathetic. Human. You fell for him, sweetie. And by the way he was looking at you, I think he fell for you, too."

———

I WIPED down the counter in the kitchen, swiping at a few nonexistent stains. There was no need, because the kitchen was already spotless. After all, no one had really been using it for the past few days. Natalie had been home so seldom that the only reason I knew she'd come back at all was because her toothbrush had been there one day and then gone the next.

She'd obviously found somewhere else to stay.

The thought of her moving out sent me into a panic. Initially, I'd been the one staying away from the apartment. After my conversation with Professor Washington, I'd decided that giving Natalie some space before we talked was the right way to go. I could explain my future plans in a calm, rational manner before we decided how to move forward.

I couldn't leave her alone, even though it was probably the best course of action for us both. I'd been climbing the walls wondering where she was just after the first twenty-four hours. There was no way I could let her go completely. But I'd figured that if we talked and everyone had the same expectations, we could go forward without anyone getting hurt. I'd still be leaving after graduation, sure, but that was a while away, and maybe we could get our fill of this insane sexual connection in the meantime.

I ignored the part of me that railed at the thought of reducing what we had to sex. After I hadn't seen her the second day, and then the third, I had gotten my first glimpse of what life after Natalie would be like. And it wasn't pretty.

I'd tried working on one of my projects and hadn't been able to concentrate. At work, I'd given three people the wrong drinks before I realized what I was doing. I'd even been called out for daydreaming in class today. I was a mess.

How could I have thought that staying away from Natalie was the best option?

It was easier to pretend that it was just sex, and that I wasn't inexplicably drawn to her. But it was useless, really, because I already knew that it was way more than the physical that was drawing us together. It was her sweetness and her smiles. It was the warmth she seemed to exude like sunlight. Just a few days without her, and I could barely function.

Nothing seemed to matter when I didn't have her face to come home to. I was startling to realize that I'd come to rely on that, knowing that she was there waiting for me, making my apartment feel like a home.

I pulled out my phone and called her again. I wasn't surprised when she didn't answer. I needed to figure out where she was and go to her. But the only person who would know was her aunt, and Professor Washington definitely wasn't going to help me.

Then I glanced over at the whiteboard where her friend Alex's number was still scrawled. Before I had time to second guess it, I dialed the number.

"Hello?"

"Is this Alex?"

"Yes, who is this?"

"It's Trevor. Natalie's roommate. Please don't hang up."

There was a sigh on the other end, and that was enough to tell me that he'd guessed correctly. She'd obviously told the other man what had happened, or he wouldn't sound so disgusted with me.

"Can I help you?" Alex's voice was cold as ice. He sounded like he really wanted to say, *Can I push you off a cliff?*

"I just need to know that Natalie is okay. Is she there?"

"Mmm. I'm not sure I want to help you."

I gritted my teeth. I needed to be nice. Alex was quite possibly the only person I knew who'd seen Natalie in the past few days.

"Please. I fucked up, but it's not what it looked like. I just want to apologize to her. Is she there?"

After a few seconds, Alex sighed. "Yes, she's here studying. Do you want to talk to her?"

Making a split-second decision, I decided to surprise her. I didn't want to give her too much time to put her guard up before I could explain.

"No, don't tell her. I want to surprise her."

"Okay, but don't take too long. I'm not a good liar, so if she asks me what's up, I won't be able to hide it."

I hung up and grabbed my keys after sticking my feet into the jogging sneakers next to the door. I was still wearing the sweatpants I'd slept in, and hadn't shaved in two days, but I was taking Alex at his word. I couldn't afford to waste any time, so I could only hope she wouldn't hold my appearance against me.

What was a guy supposed to look like when he realized he'd met the woman of his dreams, anyway? I was having an epiphany, surely I deserved to catch a break for looking a little sloppy.

When I arrived at the address Alex texted, I knew as soon as the other man opened the door that something was wrong.

"You look guilty," I accused.

Alex sighed. "I told you I wasn't a good liar. When she asked me who was on the phone, I tried to say it was my mom, but she saw right through it. Then she took my phone and looked at the call log." He rubbed his arm. "She's stronger than I expected, too."

I groaned. "Great. Do you know where she went?"

Alex shook his head. Then he glanced behind him. "You can still come in if you want. Maybe I can make you feel better?"

"Seriously?" I had to laugh at the shameless pickup line. It was either laugh or give in to the overwhelming urge to punch the other guy for letting Natalie leave so easily.

Alex held up his hands in apology, but didn't look the slightest bit sorry. "Too soon? Okay, it was worth a try."

I left, deciding that maybe the universe was giving him a hint. If Natalie didn't want to talk to me, I had to respect that.

But it didn't mean I had to like it.

15

I found a quiet corner in the library, and tossed my backpack onto the floor before plopping down on the oversized seat. I hadn't exactly been running away from Trevor, but the last thing I wanted to do was stick around and hear his excuses.

What girl really wanted to hear about how she wasn't good enough, how she was fine to sleep with, but once that fascination was over, he was done. *Nope.*

Frankly, I was pretty damn tired of guys not choosing me. This whole Trevor thing came out of the blue. I hadn't even been looking for a guy. But there he'd been, with his freaking eight-pack abs, chiseled jaw, and sinful tongue.

And you fell for it, like an idiot.

Just like I had with Brian.

Well, I was done being an idiot now. And, for that matter, I was done hiding. I was going to go back home and put my focus on where it should've been from the get-go. I'd come to Boston for a fresh start, to get away from my previous mistakes. My psychology program was top notch. I had some opportunities for some awesome internships. And for the last few weeks, I'd been focused on this guy. I didn't come here looking for a boyfriend.

You are not that girl.

No, I wasn't. And I was going to refocus, starting now. There'd be no more thinking about Trevor Hamilton. There would be no more listening to him in the shower as he moaned my name. From this point forward, I was all work, all the time.

This was going to be easy.

No. *No, it wouldn't be.* As a matter of fact, it was likely going to hurt...*a lot*. At first, anyway. But I was tough. If I'd survived Brian and his constant lying, I could survive this.

I cracked open a book and forced myself to read. It was time to focus on myself. And that's just what I was going to do.

———

THINGS around the apartment were tense. For the last two weeks, Natalie and I seemed to be two ships passing in the night.

Yeah, okay, some of that was deliberate on my part. Okay, a *lot* of that had been deliberate on my part. But after I'd gone looking for her at Alex's, I'd tried to fix it.

Fat lot of good that did me.

The problem was, I missed her. The one time I'd seen her in the hallway and tried to engage her in conversation, she'd looked through me and acted as if I wasn't there. A couple of days ago, I'd seen her laptop open to *Rent to Me*, the apartment-finder roommate site.

What the hell was I going to do if she left? This was impossible. Yeah, I'd fucked up. And I had no idea what to do about it. She wouldn't talk to me, she wouldn't look at me. The stress was affecting me. It made it hard to study, hard to concentrate.

The crazy thing was, I was more affected by this than when Courtney left. With Courtney, I really hadn't thought much of anything.

When I'd come home to find her things gone, it had been more like a "let's just get back to work" situation. All I'd had to do was turn my attention to work and it was easy to forget her. I couldn't do that with Natalie. She'd infiltrated every aspect of my daily life.

I wanted to hear her laughing as she talked with Alex on the phone. I wanted to watch her as she mouthed the lines to bad movies. I looked forward to her little notes on Tupperware containers. I liked her bad singing when she tried to do her own rendition of pop songs and replaced all the words with ones of her own.

You're a fucking mess. Yeah, tell me some shit I didn't know.

I had it bad, and right now I would do just about anything to have her back. Professor Washington had been right about one thing. With Courtney, I had been hyper-focused on my job search. On my career. I hadn't put enough into that relationship, and she eventually got sick of it.

Having Natalie here was like a breath of fresh air. Once, everything in my life had been so tightly controlled. Now, everything didn't fit into a neat little box anymore. And while I'd first thought that would kill me, it didn't. In fact, I liked it.

I wanted to figure things out with Natalie. We could work it out. Whatever it was, whatever happened. I wasn't putting my career on the back burner, I was taking a more holistic look at my life. Just like I didn't want my sister Talia to be lonely and only focus on school, I needed to take my own advice and balance the professional and personal aspects.

I wanted Natalie. More than that, I wanted to be *with* her. I needed her. I had spent way too much time dicking around over the last two weeks. Trying to fight whatever it was that I was feeling. How much time had I wasted?

I needed a break from my books, so I closed them all and headed out into the living room. The lights were almost all out, except the one I'd left on in the kitchen. Natalie was probably out again, looking for a new apartment.

Did you have to be such a dick?

Good question. No, I didn't have to be such a dick, I'd willingly chosen to be and pushed away the one girl who got me. I grabbed a beer from the kitchen and didn't even bother turning on the lights in the living room, but instead parked it on the couch and grabbed the remote. One of the movies from her collection was still in the Blu-ray player. I turned it on, needing some kind of connection to her.

Because you need help. Yeah, I did.

On the screen, Segal had a great action sequence that made

it look like he was doing no work at all. In all likelihood, *he* probably wasn't. By the time he'd filmed this one, he was a lot older. So chances were good that I was seeing a stunt double. It didn't matter though. I still loved it.

"I'm never going to find another girl that appreciates you the way I do, Segal."

"If only you'd appreciated the girl in front of you."

I whirled around, nearly spilling my beer. "Natalie. You're home."

She nodded. "Yeah, I got back an hour ago."

That tightness in my chest, the pressure that I'd been lugging along with me over the last couple of weeks, eased and dissipated for the first time in a while. I felt like I could breathe. And I knew that was her doing. The question was, how could I fix it? How could I make this better? How could I have her in my life?

I licked my lips and said the only thing I could think of, the only common ground we had right now. Inclining my head toward the TV, I asked softly, "Want to watch with me?"

I sat on the couch next to Trevor, wondering if I was making a mistake. I'd been doing so well avoiding him, but when I'd heard the unmistakable sounds of a Segal movie, I hadn't been able to stay away.

Damn him and his wonderfully horrible taste in movies.

"I've missed you," Trevor said, without looking at me.

His eyes stayed glued to the television where Segal was currently fighting several bad guys with nothing more than a lead pipe and a shoe. He spoke so softly that I wondered if he'd really meant for me to hear that. But his words didn't even make sense. I wasn't the one who'd messed everything up and then walked away. All I'd done was try to salvage the remains of my heart and pride.

"You haven't had time to miss me yet. I'm still here."

He turned then. "No, you're not here where it counts. And I really don't want you to leave. I saw you looking at that apartment-finder site. Please don't move out. I just got used to having a roommate."

I sighed. It didn't make sense that he was trying to guilt trip me. He was the one who'd brought some girl home knowing I'd be there. Maybe he should ask Jenny to move in so he could have his harem on site.

"Trevor, what did you think was going to happen? That I would just go to my room and ignore it when you bring your skanks home? No, thank you."

"No, that's not what I expected to happen. I had no idea she was coming over because I didn't invite her. There's nothing going on with Jenny. She's just a girl who asked me to tutor her."

"She was wearing a pretty obvious push-up bra for a tutoring session."

"I wouldn't know because I've never gotten near her bra. You have to believe me."

I wanted to believe him, but I was done being played for a

fool. If it looked shady, it probably was. I wasn't going to be taken off-guard by a man's infidelity again.

"Then your aunt came by and reminded me that I'm pursuing international opportunities after I graduate. I didn't think it was fair to you to start a relationship knowing that I plan to leave."

Wait, what?

My aunt had come here and talked Trevor out of dating me? I didn't know what to think of that. Aunt Patty had never been the type to be overly pushy or interfere in my life before. But the more I thought about it, it kind of made sense. My aunt knew I'd just gotten out of a bad relationship with a guy who didn't plan on sticking around. Maybe she thought she was protecting me.

But I didn't need anyone else making decisions for me. That was the main thing I'd learned over the past year. I wanted to be in control of my own life. And I wasn't going to let anyone else dictate what I did or didn't do.

"Okay, I didn't know that Aunt Patty did that. She shouldn't have told you that. I was hurt before, so she's overprotective, but I can make my own decisions. And I wanted to be with you. And you just left like that didn't matter at all."

No longer watching the movie, Trevor took my hand and brought it to his mouth. The soft kiss in my palm made me smile.

"I only stayed away because I thought it was better than having to leave later. But if I'm a wreck after just a few days, there's no way I can handle leaving you later. I need you, Natalie."

Happiness bloomed and I thought I'd burst from the sudden emotion. "So that's the solution. You can just never leave me."

Trevor smiled against my hand. "I guess so. You've bewitched me with your great taste in movies."

"This might even be a good thing, you know?" When Trevor looked at me curiously, I stood and then settled myself on his lap, straddling him.

"I've always wanted to travel, too. It would be kind of cool to have a boyfriend who lived in Europe so I could come visit."

"Do you really think that could work?" Trevor watched me with serious eyes.

"You've never heard of long distance relationships? Hello, you're a tech guy. Surely you've discovered the benefits of video chatting by now. Besides, it's not like you'd be gone forever."

Trevor grabbed me suddenly and I laughed in delight as he buried his face in my chest. "I really thought I was doing the right thing. But screw that. I need you with me, Natalie. Whatever happens, we'll find a way to make it work. Because I love you too much to let you go."

I blinked back tears. "I love you too much to let you get away. Now let's see if you can make it up to me."

———

Jesus, I had missed him.

All I wanted were Trevor's hands on me, sliding over my skin, making me hot and tingly. He ducked his head down and sucked on my neck as I let out a low moan. His hand tightened on my hips, and he seemed to revel in the sound that I made, giving me open-mouthed kisses along my neck and jaw, before finally nipping gently at my bottom lip.

I rocked my hips over the ridge of his erection, and he hissed before pressing his tongue between my lips and into my mouth. I'd missed this. I'd missed that dizzying feeling he could instill within me. It felt like the rush of the wildest roller coaster, along with the best kind of electrical zap.

In seconds, we were shoving at each other's clothes. Trevor slid his hands up my torso, gently skimming my breasts with his thumbs, before helping me tug my shirt over my head. I didn't care where the damn thing landed. I was simultaneously trying to drag his T-shirt over his head.

With a smirk, he helped me out and reached behind him, grabbing two fistfuls of material before pulling it over his dark curls.

While he worked that out, I only let myself get momentarily distracted by the display of muscles before going for his belt and unbuckling the brass.

Trevor wasted no time with his T-shirt, tossing it somewhere near the dining room table. With his hands tucking under my skirt, I cursed soft and low when his knuckles brushed over my sex.

"I'm sorry," he whispered.

With a frown, I asked, "For what?"

His fingertips snuck into the edge of my panties, and then he twisted. "For this." With a flick of his wrist, he snapped my thong.

The shock and sting of pain was quickly replaced by the

warmth and pleasure of his hands running over my skin, soothing away the hurt. "Trevor," I gasped.

He shrugged. "I said I was sorry."

He kissed me again, licking into my mouth, even as he slicked his thumb over my clit. Good Lord, it was impossible to think at all when he did that. Anytime he had his hands on me, my brain just took a hiatus.

There was some shifting and wiggling, a couple of curses, but we managed to work his jeans and boxers down to at least mid thigh so that we could free his cock together. When I reached between us and wrapped my hands around him, Trevor threw his head back into the couch cushions and cursed low, his hand digging into my hips. "Jesus, fuck me."

I chuckled. "I think I'm getting to that."

I slid both hands over his satin smooth skin, and then used my thumb to spread the drop of liquid that pooled at the tip. I marveled at how he could be so hard but so soft at the same time.

"I like how you feel," I whispered as he pushed himself further into my hands.

When he spoke, his voice was strained, more of a low growl really. "I love how you make me feel."

Trevor's brows knit, but his hips rocked upwards, pushing him further into my hands. "Please don't fucking stop. I've imagined this a million times."

"Well, you don't have to imagine anymore."

One of his hands finally released my hip and slid up my torso, stroking his thumb over my nipple through the lace of my bra. Trevor smirked when I had to halt all motion to focus on the wave of lust rushing through me.

"I love how responsive you are. One day soon, I want to see if you can come from me doing nothing else but this. Just pinching your nipples, licking them, biting them."

I shivered. I wanted that, too. But right now, there was something else I wanted more. I raised myself up on my knees and positioned him at my cleft. One hand stroking down to the root of his cock, I held him still before gently swiveling my hips, coating the tip of him.

"Jesus. Natalie. Oh my God." As if he couldn't help himself, his hips rocked into me. The first inch of him slid inside me easily.

I threw my head back and held perfectly still. "Oh my God." Yeah, I could come like this. With just the tip of him inside me. I felt full, stretched, and oh so heavenly.

"Fuck, you feel good." Trevor mumbled, then pinched my nipple harder.

I gasped. That motion alone sent my body down another inch over the thick length of him. "Trevor. God, you feel so—"

He shoved a hand into my hair and gripped tight. The sting of pain had me opening my eyes and focusing on him. "Natalie. We can't—the condoms are in my bedroom."

I licked my lips before biting down and rocking my hips a little bit more, taking more of him inside me. "You feel so good, though."

Trevor panted, sliding in just a little bit more, and then retreating an inch. The glide and pressure made me tingle. "Natalie. Listen to me. We need to stop. This isn't safe. And—"

I wasn't listening. I wanted more of him. I wanted *all* of him. Forcing my eyelids open, I said, "I'm on the pill. I started right when I moved here. Not that I anticipated this, but—"

His green eyes went dark suddenly, and he gripped my hips again, his fingertips pressing deep into my skin as he slid all the way home. With my skirt bunched up around my waist, he watched intently where we were joined. As he made love to me, he muttered words of need and longing and love.

I arched and leaned back so I could brace myself on his knees. That new position gave him all the access he needed.

One hand reached behind me, unsnapped my bra, and then shoved the lace cups up. He leaned over my body, sucking one stiff nipple into his mouth, and groaned against my breast. His other hand slid between our bodies, pressing slow, easy circles on my clit.

I was coming in seconds. Flying high and clamping around his dick. But he wasn't done. Trevor kept going. Snapping his hips forward and making me gasp and widen my eyes when he hit that magical place deep inside. And then he would retreat. With each snap of his hips, I couldn't help but call out his name.

As my orgasm coursed through me, sending my body into wicked convulsions, Trevor growled and pulled me forward on his lap. He slid his lips over mine and pressed his tongue into my mouth, kissing me deep. The top of my pelvis rubbed along his, prolonging the pleasure.

I held tight onto his shoulders as he kissed me, my hips still working, my body still taking him deep.

This was perfection.

Trevor dragged his lips off mine and kissed along my jaw,

whispering to me, making me hotter. "So fucking beautiful... I could do this all damn day... You feel so good..."

His hand fisted in my hair more gently than before, while the other slid over my ass, rocking me more firmly against him as he loved me. When he slid a finger down the seam of my ass, I hesitated for only a moment, but then relaxed against him.

I trusted him. I loved him. I was his to do with what he wanted.

When his finger pressed against my pucker, the first sensation was shock, and then astonishment at the sting of pleasure. But when he eased a finger gently inside, I broke apart again, pushing myself up onto my knees and slamming back down over him.

Trevor held perfectly still, his muscles going rigid. As he came, his gaze didn't leave mine, and he sank home one more time. "I am never letting you go. We belong together."

I sank over him once more, and we both groaned, riding the wave of the last vestiges of our orgasms.

He might never let me go, but more importantly, I never wanted to leave. This was where I belonged.

In his arms.

DYING to know how Trevor took the news about Talia & Cage? We'll send it to you FREE!

EXCERPT OF SHAMELESS

AVAILABLE EVERYWHERE

I am the thing that goes bump in the night. I am a liar, a protector ... a killer ... I am Noah Blake.

There is only one light in my darkness. one bright ray in the storm of my life. Lucia DeMarco. And I'll do anything for her. Anything except show her who I really am: an assassin. Well, former assassin. I don't really do that anymore ... usually.

It would be easier if she didn't call me names. Asshole, control freak ... shameless. It would also be easier if she didn't look at me with those trusting gray eyes. If I didn't dream about the perfect curve of her — Never mind all that. The point is she's digging into my world, my secrets, and it's going to get her killed.

But first, we have another more immediate concern. Lucia is going on a *date*—with someone else ...

And I'm not allowed to kill this one.

Excerpt of Shameless © May 2017 M. Malone and Nana Malone

———

Noah watched the date from the comfort of his SUV. All the while silently fuming.

What the hell did Lucia think she was doing? His team hadn't vetted the guy. They didn't know anything about him. So far, she'd broken all of the dating rules he'd given her.

For the first date, always meet your date at your designated location. And of course, she'd let this doofus pick her up for their date. As if he hadn't told her a million times to do the exact opposite.

He'd also been very clear not to get in the car with her date. So that was rule one and rule two broken right off the bat. As if he hadn't trained her on how to be careful and what to watch out for. But *oh no*, Lucia didn't listen to shit. Every time he turned around, there she was, careening headfirst into trouble.

Maybe she didn't see her date as a potential threat, but dammit she needed to be more careful. What the hell did she even know about this guy?

"What the hell kind of name is Brent anyway?"

Noah hadn't even realized that he'd spoken out loud, until the voice in his comm unit laughed. "Last I checked, Brent is a perfectly normal name. Lots of guys have it."

Noah barely restrained a growl. "Matthias, when I want your input, I'll give it to you."

There was a chuckle on the other end of the line. Noah made a mental note to give Matthias some really horrible surveillance duty for the next month. This wasn't funny. This was Lucia. They all cared about her well-being.

Maybe you more than the others.

Yeah, so what? He cared about her. And maybe it wasn't the easiest thing in the world watching her date loser after loser. But it was his job, no strike that, it was his *responsibility* to look after her. He owed Rafe that much. But how the hell was he supposed to look out for her when she kept making it so damn difficult? Lucia was obstinate, infuriating, pigheaded, and—

Beautiful.

No. She was like a little sister to him. Yet somehow his dick couldn't seem to get with that program lately. More and more frequently, some very *unsisterly* thoughts wormed their way into his consciousness.

"Matthias, give me something on this Brent guy. Aren't you supposed to be some kind of super-hacker?"

"You better believe it. But, there's nothing on him. Everything is normal. Boring. Most interesting thing about this guy is he likes adventure sports. He skydives, bungee jumps, that sort of thing. Does some triathlons. Maybe he's some kind of adrenaline junkie. But there's nothing else on him. No flags. He lives here in New York in the East Village. No roommates, rent isn't exorbitant. Works for the city. No large withdrawals of cash, good credit. As far as I can tell, he's clean. But that's just his electronic trail. Maybe you're right on this one and he's a little too clean. I mean, there's not even an online dating profile on him. To me, that's weird. Who doesn't have an online dating profile?"

Noah chuckled and then lifted his binoculars again. Lucia was laughing at something. So Brent thought he was a comedian, huh? What the hell was so damn funny? There was too much interference to use the boom mic, otherwise he'd know.

Brent reached across the table and took Lucia's hand, and Noah nearly chipped a tooth from grinding his teeth so hard. He could see Lucia's eyes go wide. Was that surprise? He hoped it was disgust.

Did she actually like this guy?

His gut clenched at the thought. Perfect, just what he needed. Lucia liking this fucking idiot.

It wasn't that she hadn't dated before. She had. Mostly in college. Most of those guys had merely needed a strong reminder to mind their Ps & Qs with her. But this guy, this guy was random—unknown. Which meant it would take more work to scare him off. But Noah was up for the challenge.

Lucia deserved to be happy, just with somebody vetted and approved. After the shit she had survived in her life? The girl needed some happy endings.

Fuck. Not happy endings.

He groaned and turned his attention back to the restaurant. Brent raised a hand and signaled their server. Shit, they were leaving. The real trick was guessing where they were going. He'd put a tracker on her phone, so if he guessed wrong, he could always follow. But what if something happened to her before he could get there?

"Matthias, turn on the listening device on her phone. I'm heading to the house in case that's where they go."

There was a beat of silence. He could almost hear Matthias's silent condemnation. "The thing is, Noah, she's not going to like that."

"The thing is, Matthias, I don't care," he muttered using the same singsong tone.

Yeah, he knew he sounded like an asshole. But this was Lucia. If she wasn't going to take care of herself, that left it to him to do it for her. They had one simple rule: He vetted all her dates. And sometimes, without her knowing, he'd scare them off. But that was really beside the point. It wasn't his fault she couldn't pick a decent guy.

He made a left turn on 10th Ave, right near the USB Theater, then he sped through Chelsea before making a left on 28th Street, heading toward Chelsea Piers. He made a right at the stop sign, turning onto her quiet street. The street was lined with lofts and new apartment high-rises, all boasting a name with Arms, or Manor.

Before she'd moved, Noah and his team researched the building's owners and the neighborhood crime rate. Everything to make sure she would be safe. Well as safe as she could be in Manhattan. It also didn't hurt that he watched her every move. And not in some creepy, stalkery way, but more like a big brother way. *Sort of* ...

Never mind that. He drove past her building and around the back to the lot he paid for specifically for these kinds of situations. Yeah, so maybe he also paid most of her rent. She thought she'd gotten extremely lucky with a rent-controlled apartment in the heart of the city. In reality, he paid most of the tab. He also paid for two parking spots. Not that Lucia had a car. But in case she ever got one, she'd have somewhere safe to park it. Somewhere right next to the damn elevator. He paid almost as much to secure that spot as he paid for the apartment. His spot was in the darkened shadows somewhere she'd never think to look. He didn't mind though, because in most scenarios, he was the thing that went bump in the night.

"Matthias, talk to me. Where are they headed?"

"They're stopping for ice cream at Benny's then he's going to take her home."

Okay, so Noah had about ten minutes. Benny's was a local mom-and-pop ice-cream place about five blocks away. He jogged along the parking garage to the side stairs. While he'd insisted that she get a building with a doorman, there was no accounting for the additional exits and entrances into the building. Luckily, this one was exit only. Only confirmed residents had keys. Unfortunately, even your average guy could pick these locks, and he happened to be better than average.

In less than a minute, he was through the door and took the

back stairway up to her apartment. She'd listened to him and employed the deadbolt. Problem for her was he had a key.

In seconds he turned off her security alarm. Well, at least there was that. Lucia had been so against it in the first place. At least she realized that a woman living alone needed *some* security. He glanced around and noted that she'd changed a few things. Was that a new pillow?

Matthias spoke into his earpiece. "You've got about five, boss. They've stopped outside the apartment. I'm going to go ahead and turn off the mic on her phone now if that's okay with you."

More judgment from the youngest member of the team. Whatever. He'd deal with that later. Now, the real question was where to wait for her.

What if she brought the guy in here?

Oh hell no. The mere idea of it had him gripping the edge of the countertop. She had better be coming in alone.

Didn't she know the first thing about dating? Damn it, this was their first date. She was supposed to make the guy twist in the wind for a bit first.

How many one-night stands have you had?

No. He was not going to think about that. It was different. That's all. Besides, Lucia was a good kid. And there was no way Nonna DeMarco would approve.

He'd give her a few minutes to run the guy off herself, and then the two of them were going to have another conversation about dating and personal safety.

She couldn't really be interested in this guy, right? He was boring. *Unlike you?* Noah grimaced. Yeah well, she didn't need to date anyone like him either. If she did, Noah would have to employ more drastic measures to keep her safe.

No. Lucia needed a nice guy, but someone more interesting than a records keeper.

Okay, if he was going to give her the chance to send Brent packing by herself, he needed to wait somewhere other than the living room. If she caught sight of Noah first, and if she was carrying that Taser he'd given her for Christmas, he might end up as fried toast. He jogged down the hallway and turned left into her bedroom, gently closing the door behind himself.

He hopped onto her bed, bouncing slightly and leaned back against the pillows. *I've always loved how girly she is*, he thought, enjoying the scent of her perfume in the room and looking around at the four-poster bed, the soft colors, and all the ruffled pillows. He also loved that when she completely lost her temper her curls went flying and her eyes snapped with anger.

It was probably why he enjoyed pissing her off so much.

Something caught his eye as he lay back against the pillows, readjusting them for his comfort. Her bottom drawer was open.

Do not open it. Leave it be. She won't appreciate — Oh fuck it.

He pulled it open and took out his phone, shining the flashlight directly inside.

"Well, well, well. What do we have here?"

———

This was the part where Lucia was supposed to feel the butterflies right? Every brush of his fingers was supposed to feel as if she had electricity coursing through it? This was the part where she moaned into his embrace, right?

Except none of that was happening. Not even when he pulled her close, pressing their bodies together.

This was ... *Nice.* Perfectly pleasant. Maybe even a little warm. Warm was good, right?

Head in the game DeMarco.

She started slowly, leading him back toward the bedroom. Maybe if she got him there she'd get more in the mood. She'd have all the nice-smelling girly things in there which hopefully would feel more romantic.

He easily followed her lead. He made a moaning sound deep in his throat, and she only wished she wanted to make such a sound. A tiny annoying voice spoke up from deep in the recesses of her mind.

Are you sure you want to do this? You want your first time to just be ... fine?

No. She wanted hot. She wanted sexy. She wanted to tingle. She wanted to feel like a supermodel who'd found her accompanying rock star. But not everybody got a rock star. Sometimes nice was good.

She opened the door to the bedroom, and he continued to kiss her. But the more his tongue slid into her mouth, licking inside, the more she wanted to turn her head. She drew back, angling her head away slightly. He took that to mean that she wanted him to kiss her neck. With a little groan, he slid his lips along her jaw, then the column of her throat. But she was having a hard time getting into the mood.

All she kept thinking about was if she was doing this right. And God, she wanted to get out of her shoes. They were pinching her toes. And those growling noises he was making were actually kind of funny. When had she left her blinds open? While she was at it, she really needed to get some damn groceries.

This is not what you're supposed to be thinking about. There was something wrong with her. He was a perfectly nice guy wanting to rock her world. And she was thinking about her damn blinds and groceries.

I bet you wouldn't feel this way with Noah.

And just like that, heat raced through her bloodstream and her breath caught. Just thinking about him was enough to make her skin tight and itchy. Those butterflies she'd been concerned about, there they were, fluttering rapidly inside, making something deep in her core pull tight.

Still, Lucia fought it. There was no way she was going to think about Noah at a time like this. But, maybe that wasn't the end of the world. It was just a fantasy. Her brain latched on to what her body was craving. And the image of him in her mind formed and solidified.

Suddenly, it wasn't Brent kissing her throat, it was Noah. But his lips weren't quite as soft. They were firm. Sure. Knew exactly what he wanted and exactly how to get the right response from her.

There was no thinking about anything else when she was with him. Only the sensation of being in his arms. The sensation of her heart hammering so fast it nearly beat out of her chest. The feeling she sometimes got when he looked at her and all her bones felt like jelly. That was how it was meant to be with Noah.

A little dangerous. Definitely bad for you. But oh so good.

Lucia slid her hands into Noah's hair, tugging a little. He muttered a soft curse against her throat, his hands holding her flush against him. Through his jeans she could feel the pulse of his erection against her center.

Yes. This was much more like it.

His kisses grew more frantic. His hands less patient. They skimmed over her hips with a strong grip. Before sliding his thumbs up over her belly and over her ribcage, just under her —

"Okay, Romeo. I think that's enough."

Lucia squeaked, then jumped away from Noah — err, Brent. *Right Brent.* Her date. Noah, the idiot, was on her bed.

"Wha–What the hell are you doing here, Noah?"

Noah lay back against her pillows. His feet were on her bed with his shoes on, she noticed with irritation. He looked comfortable. Completely relaxed, as if he belonged there. *Wouldn't you like that?*

"Well, it looks like I'm just in time to interrupt."

Brent stared between her and Noah, then back again. "I thought you said you didn't have a boyfriend."

Lucia turned her attention to him and placed a reassuring hand on his arm. "I don't. The intruder on my bed is my wannabe big brother. *And he was just leaving.*"

Noah shook his head. "No such luck, princess. You don't know this dude from a can of paint. We had a deal. You let me check out anyone you want to go out with. You seem to have forgotten that."

"We never had a deal. You just seem to think that you can dictate to me. You can't!"

Brent interjected. "I should probably be going."

Lucia gripped his forearm harder. "No. Stay. Noah is going. Aren't you Noah?"

Noah grinned, his devilish smile bringing a mischievous

twinkle to his eyes. Looking at the two of them in close proximity, Lucia could see clearly that there was no competition. Noah had dark sooty lashes that framed those intense whiskey-colored eyes, high cheekbones, a straight Roman nose, and full lips that tilted crookedly when he smiled. The man was gorgeous and he knew it. Which was a problem, because he often used it to get what he wanted.

Brent, in comparison, also had dark hair, but not as dark as Noah's. It also didn't fall in disarray where some parts looked styled and other parts unkempt, but mostly looking like he'd just rolled out of bed. Or he'd rolled out of bed *with someone*. Brent's eyes were a pale blue. Kind. He was cute in that boy-next-door, all-American kind of way. He didn't look like he belonged in a fashion magazine, not like Noah did.

Feeling a little uncharitable for comparing Brent so unfavorably with Noah, she had to concede that he was at least tall. Not as tall as Noah, but few men could compare to Noah's towering height. Besides it wasn't about looks, or height, or charisma, anyway.

Annoyed with herself, Lucia closed her eyes, hoping maybe this was all a bad dream, but when she opened them again he was still there. With Noah in the room, it was hard to breathe. He dominated everyone and sucked up all the air, silently pulling her towards him with his gravitational force alone. It was like poor Brent wasn't even there.

"Now, Lucia, I know you'd like to think you're in charge right now. But you're not. You don't know this guy. And you invited him back to your place? I thought I taught you better than that."

Brent tried to make an escape again. "Lucia, why don't you deal with this guy? And we'll try this again later."

"No. You're not going anywhere."

Noah pushed himself to a seated position on the edge of the bed. "Oh yes he is. Because you and I need to discuss what the hell this is for." He held up the party gift from the bachelorette party.

Oh no. Oh no. Oh no.

In that moment, Lucia prayed to every saint her grandmother had ever forced her to pray to. Prayed to the Virgin Mary then to Jesus. Heck, for good measure she added Buddha in there too. Just in case. But nothing happened. The ground did not open and swallow her.

Instead, she stood with her hand on Brent's arm, staring at Noah as he held up the largest purple dildo she'd ever seen in her life.

Brent's mouth fell open but no sound came out. As mortified as she was, Lucia couldn't really blame him. The stupid thing was over a foot long, and thick. Really, really thick. Like thicker than a cucumber. She'd certainly never used the thing. It was a gag gift.

"How dare you go through my things!" she squeaked.

Noah shrugged. "I didn't go through your things. The drawer was open. The thing was practically sticking out of it. Making its escape."

Next to her, Brent shifted his gaze to her.

"That's not mine," she whispered. "I m-mean it is but I've never used it. It's a gag gift from a bachelorette party." She swung her gaze to Noah. "*Put that down.*"

"Not a chance. I mean, this thing is fascinating. I'm no stranger to toys myself. As far as I'm concerned, they can always enhance the situation. I'm not one of those guys that feel jealous or threatened. Matter of fact, I'm all for a little solo play. But this thing..." He held it up and shook it around. "Even I've never seen anything like it. And I've had a lot of practice."

He turned his attention to Brent. "No disrespect to you, but I don't think you can live up to this. It vibrates *and* rotates! Even I feel a little frightened by this thing."

Screw the ground opening up and swallowing her whole. Just shoot her now. That would end this quickly. Shoot her. Send her little behind to heaven. Because she was done. Noah was bending the dildo around as it wiggled in his hands. He pushed the button, and the damn thing rotated on its own, making a whirring sound. *Oh God.* Could this get any worse?

Brent fixed his gaze on her. "I'm going to go."

"No, please don't go."

She lunged and grabbed at the dildo, tugging when Noah refused to release it. The silicone material bent in ways Lucia was sure it wasn't designed to as they fought over it. This was easily one of the most undignified moments of her life, but she just couldn't take it anymore. Noah's smug face as he watched her struggling to get a better grip on the wiggling, gyrating piece of plastic only made it worse.

"Ugh, let go!"

In a fit of sudden anger, Lucia kicked him in the shin. And in his surprise, Noah let go of his end of the toy. The next few seconds would forever play in her mind in slow motion as she watched the toy fly end over end and hit Brent directly in the face.

"Ouch!"

Lucia covered her mouth in horror as the toy fell to his feet. The silence that followed was only broken by the sounds of the still-running toy, wiggling over the carpet.

Noah guffawed. "My bad. Did I get it in your mouth? Don't worry, it doesn't mean anything. What's a little dick in the mouth between friends, am I right?"

"I have to go."

"No, wait!"

But Brent didn't wait. All she could hear were his footsteps as they echoed on the hardwood floors, down the hall, into her living room, then kitchen, and then the front door opening and slamming shut behind him.

With a deep breath, Lucia whirled on Noah.

"I swear to God I will make you pay if it's the last thing I do. You are going to pay so hard. What the hell is wrong with you? *You are completely shameless!*"

He grinned as he stood and then knelt to grab the toy,

pushing the button on the dildo again. "I'm looking forward to it. This is the best laugh I've had in months."

He moved towards her, his gait smooth and predatory. He paused about a foot away, and she could smell the scent of sandalwood. She fought the urge to inhale deeply.

When he leaned close, Lucia held her breath.

"Next time, *I* check out the guy. And pick somebody tougher. If he'd stood up to me, I would have respected him more."

Lucia couldn't help it. Frustration was taking over as the blood boiled under her skin. And the urge to hit him overwhelmed her.

"I hate you."

He took a step, bringing them so close they were almost touching. When he leaned over her again, she nervously licked her lips as her belly flipped.

His voice was low and sultry as he whispered. "No. You don't."

Read Shameless now at malonesquared.com/shameless

EXCERPT OF WICKED

AVAILABLE IN KINDLE UNLIMITED

Get WICKED now at malonesquared.com/wicked

What could be worse than catching your creepy boss in an inappropriate position? *Hearing him say your name.*

Bailey

This day couldn't get any worse.

I just saw my boss Mr. Dent's extremely unimpressive... dent. A night of drinking with my best friend is exactly what I need. Hunter is always there for me. The perfect Mr. Nice Guy.

Hunter

This day couldn't get any better.

Finally I get my chance to show my best friend that I'm also the best guy for her. I just saw Bailey's perfect curves soaped up in the shower and all my dreams are coming true. Until she won't return my calls the next day.

Bailey wants to pretend none of it happened but I just need one chance to prove our attraction is real. I'm finally going to show her that I'm not that...nice.

Excerpt of WICKED © July 2018 M. Malone and Nana Malone

Bailey

One year later...

I smiled to myself as yet another text came through.

Hunter: Get your ass down here now

It was Friday night and the rest of the office had already knocked off to go down to Happy's, the bar right down the street from our building. It was our favorite spot for happy hour, thanks to the cheap drinks and terrible music. I'd be right there with them if I hadn't gotten so behind on my work today.

Or if my asshole boss hadn't dumped project busy work on me just a few hours ago. I wasn't even assigned to any of these projects specifically. Who did that?

Hunter: Charles from Legal is on the bar dancing. I think he's trying to twerk.

I snorted at the mental image of the older man trying to shake his ass. Our firm was a pretty conservative place and when I'd first started interning here, I'd been really intimidated. Everyone seemed so busy and professional, like they all had their shit together, while I was just trying to figure out what I wanted to do after college. But this was my second summer interning with the company and after a few Friday nights hanging out with the office crew, I'd discovered that even the most conservative types had a wild side.

Not that I wanted to picture the nice older man who always helped me with legal questions trying to gyrate his nonexistent ass. I giggled at just the thought.

Hunter: Seriously, where the hell are you?

Fed up, I finally responded. Damn, he could be such a drama king sometimes.

Me: Trying to finish all this work Mr. D gave me at the last minute. I could finish faster if you'd stop texting me!

I returned to my computer screen and squinted at the small column of numbers. I sighed. Numbers weren't my thing. I'd thought I was safe by majoring in marketing, but apparently even marketing majors needed to know how to adhere to a budget for their projects. My boss, Mr. Dent, didn't really seem to understand the budget all that well himself, though. Probably why he'd dumped this on me at the last minute.

After making a few minor changes to the numbers I'd entered earlier, I saved the file to the project drive and printed. It wasn't perfect, but it was the best I could do. What the hell could he really expect at the last minute on a Friday? It was already eight o'clock, and no one else had stayed this late. If I was lucky, Mr. Dent had fallen asleep at his desk again, and I could just slide this into his inbox without having to interact with him.

I hated having to talk to my creepy older boss, a man who still thought a comb over was preferable to just being bald, especially when there was no one else there to act as a buffer. It wasn't any one thing he'd done that made me uncomfortable; there was just something about the way he looked at me. I shuddered as I gathered my things. He looked at me like he wished he could see through my clothes. I sighed, realizing his cringeworthy gazes were the only action I'd seen in months.

I walked down the hallway toward Mr. Dent's corner office. My handbag thumped against my thigh as I walked awkwardly, trying to type a text to Hunter at the same time. Maybe if I hadn't been distracted, I would have heard the noises before I got to the doorway.

"Oh yes, that's it. Suck that dick."

I halted in the doorway, the hand that was holding my phone going up to cover my mouth. My brain was in such shock that I tried to cover my mouth and my eyes simultaneously, but I couldn't block the grotesque image playing out right in front of me.

The light was off in the room but Mr. Dent had a large picture window right behind him and the late evening light was more than enough to illuminate what he was doing. He'd pushed his chair back from his desk and sat with his legs spread, creating more room for him as his meaty hand tugged at the short, stubby penis protruding from his pants.

I clutched my phone tighter, my mouth opening and closing in shock. I knew I should probably move, but what if he saw me from the corner of his eye? So far, he hadn't noticed me, and I definitely didn't want to do anything to draw his attention.

"Oh fuck yeah. That's it. Yes. Yes. Bailey!" He shouted my name and let out a long, agonizing groan.

His hand moved so fast it was a blur, but there was no missing the stream of white that sprayed everywhere as he continued to groan out my name.

My name.

Horrified, I backed out of the room slowly. Luckily, Mr. Dent still had his eyes squeezed closed as his hand continued to pump absently at his now deflated mini-sausage. There was an expression of complete and total satisfaction on his face.

OhmyGodOhmyGodOhmyGod.

My heart was practically beating out of my chest as I trotted down the hallway, my phone still clutched in my hand. What the hell was that? Had he actually said my name?

I squeezed my eyes shut as a wave of revulsion swept through me. The elevator was right in front of me, but I was scared to hit the button. What if he heard me? Then I thought, *Fuck it*, and hit the button to call the elevator. If he hadn't heard me running down the hallway, then I was probably safe.

The entire walk over to Happy's, I replayed the last five minutes. It felt like a nightmare I couldn't wake up from. This was my boss! I had to go back to work on Monday and look him in the eye like nothing had happened! I almost gagged just thinking about all the times he'd come up behind me at my desk and put his hand on my shoulder.

For the rest of eternity, I'd have a new image of exactly where his hands had been. *Shudder.*

Hunter texted me again. Without even reading his message, I typed back.

Me: I am traumatized. There better be a drink waiting for me when I get there.

Suddenly the phone in my hand rang. I answered with a shaky "Hello?"

"What the hell happened? Do I need to kick someone's ass?" Hunter growled.

I clutched my bag tighter as I sped up. The front door of the bar was now visible. "It's so much worse than that. I'm almost there. And Hunter?"

"Yeah, baby girl?"

"I was serious about that drink. In fact, make it two."

Hunter

The things I did for the friend that I'd been crushing on for what felt like forever...

It was hard to believe that we'd only known each other a year. She'd started interning at my company the prior summer. There was a slight age difference—she was still in college, after all. But I didn't think that twenty-six was too old. There were advantages in dating a guy who was a little older. Advantages like the ability to not come in the first five minutes of sex and knowing what the clitoris was capable of.

I had mastered both in college and was a much better man for it. If only Bailey would let me show her. But she didn't see me that way. I was the charming guy who worked a floor above hers and was always up for a coffee run, not the one she wanted to drag into the supply closet and make out with.

As soon as Bailey appeared in the doorway of the bar, I could tell something was seriously wrong. She obviously hadn't been exaggerating when she said she was traumatized. Her eyes darted around the room wildly, like she'd just seen a ghost, and her hands shook as she tried to straighten her hair. That was another clue. Bailey always looked perfect. I'd never seen her with a hair out of place, but the bun she always wore was falling down and her hair hung loosely around her neck. When she saw me, her eyes lit up, which made me feel about ten feet tall.

Bailey pushed her way through the crowd and dropped into the chair across from me. Tables were always at a premium, so there were several other people I didn't know at the other end of the table. Bailey snatched one of the vodka shots from in front of me and tossed it back. I watched in amazement as she winced and then blew out a breath. Then she reached over and took the other one, the one I'd been saving for myself, and drank that too.

"What the hell happened to you?" I finally asked.

"Oh God. I don't even know where to start." She dropped her head into her hand.

I'd seen that she texted me some random video earlier, but I hadn't had a chance to watch it because her other texts had come rushing in. Knowing Bailey, she'd probably sent me another blurry video as she walked around the office. I'd never met a person worse with technology than Bailey. She also managed to butt-dial me frequently.

Finally she leaned closer. "You can't tell anyone this. I'm serious."

I pantomimed locking my lips with a key. "I'm a vault. Come on, Bay, you know I'm not a gossip."

She leaned even closer. "I saw Mr. Dent jerking off in his office." She took a really deep breath. "And then when he... you know, *finished*... he said my name. *Several* times."

After a long moment spent staring at her, I stood and went over to the bar and held up two fingers. A few minutes later I returned to the table with two more vodka shots. I sat down and slid one across the table to Bailey, who took it gratefully.

She tilted her head back, and I watched her throat work as she swallowed.

Heat climbed my face. Damn, I was just as bad as her boss. Mr. Dent wasn't my manager, but he was the one who managed the intern program. He was a crotchety older man, the type who liked to argue just to hear the sound of his own voice. The thought of that dude wanking and fantasizing about Bailey was enough to turn my stomach, so I could only imagine how she felt. I took my own shot, hoping the alcohol could clear the image.

"Shit, you weren't kidding when you said it was traumatizing."

"Yes! Oh my God, how the hell am I supposed to go to work on Monday?" Bailey's loud screech drew some attention from the strangers at the end of their table. She shrank under their stares, lowering her voice. "And now I'm acting like the drunk crazy girl in the bar. This is just great."

Her words slurred slightly and I figured that was a sign. Bailey was a petite thing, so three vodka shots in close succession probably wasn't the best idea. But if any situation could benefit from a little alcohol-induced memory loss, this one qualified for sure.

"Come on, let's get you home." I pulled up the taxi app on my phone and called for a car. It showed one two streets away. I stood and held out my hand to Bailey.

She stood. "You don't have to do that. I appreciate you listening. I didn't mean to make you leave early." She hugged me, wrapping her arms around my waist and resting her head right over my heart.

I tried to pull back slightly so she wouldn't feel the erection that was steadily growing. She'd just seen the grossest thing imaginable, so I figured the last thing she'd want would be to come into contact with dick of any kind. But when I tried to step back, her arms tightened and she pressed her face against my shirt.

"You're such a good friend!" she wailed. Since her face was turned into my chest, it came out muffled, sounding more like "Yooof such a goob fiend!"

I sighed. "Okay, this is not going to work. Come on, baby girl." I led her to the door, walking sideways half the time since she didn't want to let go of my waist. By the time we made it through the crowd and got to the cab waiting at the curb, Bailey was barely walking on her own and her hands had decided to take a walking tour of my body. I managed to get her in the cab, ignoring the skeptical look of the driver.

"Man, is she okay? She'd better not throw up in my cab."

I shot the guy a look. "Drive fast then." I gave him Bailey's address and then jumped when I felt her hand in my lap.

I gritted my teeth as I tried to peel her fingers off my thigh.

This was typical luck for me. The girl who'd never been interested in me before was handsy when she was drunk.

Typical luck.

———

Bailey

Once Hunter had me back home, I had an even more difficult time keeping my hands to myself. *Now wait just a minute. Hunter had all this going on?* I slid my hands over his pecs and abs, silently counting the muscles. Well, well. Hunter had been holding out on me.

Okay, I wasn't an idiot: he was clearly cute. Smoking hot, from a truly objective standpoint. He had dark brown hair that I was pretty sure he styled into messy disarray. His moss green eyes were kind and intelligent, but also really expressive. I could always tell his mood by his eyes. When I'd started at Bold Horizons, a year ago, my focus had been on my future. What I did here would also get me into the MBA program.

So I'd worked hard to put thoughts of the super nice, super hot young executive out of my mind. Well, except when I was in bed, alone, with a vibrator guaranteed to make me scream.

I didn't have the best luck with guys, and I wasn't looking to make a mistake where I worked. I always chose wrong. And when it came down to it, Hunter had turned out to be a really good friend. When stuff at school was hard, I could escape into our friendship. During the school year, I commuted from campus, but since it was summer, the company had found me this corporate apartment as part of the internship program.

And now, I was here...with Hunter...and he felt so good. No, seriously, why hadn't I jumped his bones before? *Because you know how you are. Once you get close, you panic and you run.*

I knew this line of thought was entirely due to the copious amount of alcohol I'd imbibed. But there was a part of me that wanted to do this. This was *Hunter*. He was my friend. He was so sweet. Exactly the kind of guy that every girl should want to be with.

He took care of me, and did all the gentlemanly things you only read about in books. Even though we were just friends, every time he dropped me off at my apartment, he made it a point to walk me to the door and make sure I got in okay.

If he invited me somewhere, he insisted on paying. It all evened out in the end because I'd often bought the beers, but it was more than that. He listened. And whenever he had a girlfriend issue, he talked about each girl with respect. I'd never let myself admit it before, but I was always a little bit jealous.

Not because of the girls per se, because I wasn't looking for that from Hunter. *Are you sure about that?* But because of the kind of guy he was. I wanted someone like that for myself, eventually. You know, after I graduated and had my career on track. Then it would be time to find someone who wouldn't hurt me.

Except with Hunter tonight, with him holding me, I wanted him to help me forget. Forget what I'd seen and heard. *Ugh.* Please God, I really needed to forget what I'd heard.

And the more I touched Hunter, the more my brain focused on the tingling low in my belly than it did on the horrors I'd seen before I left the office.

"Hunter, how come you've never asked me out before?"

I could hear the question coming out of my mouth. It was

like my brain wasn't in control. At least not the rational part of my brain, the part that would remind me that this was *Hunter*. He was my *friend*, and not some guy that I could just anonymously sleep with and walk away from.

Hunter cleared his throat. "Well, *Bay*, because we're friends. And you've always made it pretty clear that you aren't looking to date."

"And what if I've changed my mind?" I leaned into him. "What if I think I was being an idiot? What if I *want* you to ask me out?"

I lifted my gaze to his, and his pupils dilated as his eyes dropped to my lips for a moment.

Yes. The idea of Hunter kissing me made my clit throb. I pressed closer. God, he smelled amazing. And to think about him wrapping his arms around me as he kissed me and touched me and...okay, yeah, this Hunter thing, it seemed like a pretty good idea.

I stood on tiptoes, looping my arms around his neck. "You're my best friend. You take such good care of me. I especially need that right now. You want to take care of what I need, Hunter?"

My breasts pressed into his chest and my nipples hardened.

Just being close to him and rubbing up against him lit my body on fire.

Oh, God, yes.

I licked my bottom lip, before pressing my mouth to his. For a moment, his hands tightened on my hips and he groaned low. The jolt of lust ran straight from my nipples down between my thighs.

But then something was wrong. Instead of pulling me closer so I could feel the length of him pulsing against my belly, he was pushing me...away.

"Hunter?"

He squeezed his eyes shut and clenched his jaw. "Bailey. Let's get you into bed. Pull out your pajamas or whatever and get changed. We can talk about this later. When you're sober. Because when you're sober, I am so down for having this conversation. But not now when you're trashed. Come on, off to bed."

I let him lead me down the hall to the bedroom, even as I muttered, "I like the idea of off to bed."

He chuckled low. "Bailey. Stop. I don't want you to regret anything that you say tomorrow." With an efficiency that showed he'd done this before, he unzipped my pencil skirt and then turned his back while simultaneously handing me a pair of leggings. "Put these on."

I took them from him, but then I swayed. My stomach roiled, and suddenly I didn't feel so good. "Hunter? I feel a little sick."

He whirled back around and studied me, his eyes intense. "Okay, off to the bathroom."

He carried me. Had I been sober, I would've known enough to be embarrassed. Right now, I didn't really care. When he set my feet down on the cool tile in my bathroom, I swayed again.

Hunter's hands eased into my hair, and he gently pulled the strands back off my shoulders.

Even as he tucked my hair behind my ears, my stomach screamed at me as if to say, *Bitch, next time don't have three shots of vodka. Because why?*

I meant to kneel down to the toilet, but I misjudged the distance. So when my stomach finally give up the fight, cramping and trying to eject everything I'd imbibed, I partially got the sink, but mostly I got Hunter.

Could this get any worse?

———

Hunter

Fuck me.

No, seriously, I really wished she would fuck me.

I looked up at the ceiling and inhaled deeply three times. Ever since Bailey Jones had shown up at Bold Horizons, I'd had a perpetual state of blue balls. And I was certainly going to need balls of steel to deal with this situation.

How is this even happening?

First of all, Bailey thought I was hot? From the get-go, she'd made it a point to ignore any flirting from anyone in the office. When I hadn't immediately come on to her, she'd seemed relieved, and actually become my friend.

I hadn't meant for things to work out quite that well. Yes, of course I wanted to get to know her, but I'd been trying to give her space before asking her out.

It was a new tactic for me. Normally, I had zero problems with women. I looked at them, they knew I wanted them, they smiled back, and usually approached him. Or at least, when I approached, there was no hesitation, no question. Everybody was there for the party.

But with Bailey, things were different. For starters, I worked with her, and I knew better than to shit where I ate. Even if some of the girls there were beautiful, it wasn't worth the hassle.

Secondly, I *liked* her. She was smart, funny, and had this way of putting me completely at ease. She didn't take herself too seriously. It didn't matter how shitty my day was; the moment she smiled, or laughed, or started telling me some ridiculous story, I immediately relaxed. If anything went wrong in my life, Bailey was my first call. Somehow, the girl I'd been trying to sleep with had become my best friend. I had it bad.

Someone was coming for my player card any moment now.

Deal with the problem at hand. Right now, Bailey was trashed. Completely and totally obliterated. Oh, and she'd thrown up all over me, so there was that. A shower was needed for both of us. How the hell was I going to manage this?

I gritted my teeth. "Bay, we need to get in the shower."

She sloppily grinned up at me. "Now you're talking."

Oh hell. The things she was saying. If I didn't know better, I'd think she wanted me. But no, she was drunk. Bailey with all her sober senses would never say any of these things. Didn't matter though, my dick was harder than iron.

Apparently, even though I knew she didn't mean it, my dick hadn't gotten with the program. I was here to be best-friend Hunter. Not I-want-to-fuck-you-in-the-shower-up-against-the-wall-until-you-scream-my-name Hunter. *That* Hunter was on hiatus. At least for Bailey, he was.

Oh, I dated, but casually. *Very* casually. Because I usually found the women I went out with lacking within one or two dates. After all, they weren't Bay. Dammit, I had a real problem.

My dick twitched as if to say, *Damn straight, you do.*

I sighed. "Bay, you're going to finish getting undressed. Can you cooperate with me while we get this done?"

She nodded at me and gave me a happy smile. God, that smile. Sometimes it was the most perfect thing about my day.

I shed my clothes, but left on my boxer briefs. Next came the rest of Bailey's clothing. I did the best I could without looking.

Her stockings nearly did me in. She was wearing thigh highs with delicate lace at the top. I knew the memory of peeling those down her long legs would be forever imprinted in my spank bank.

Once she tossed away her blouse, she stood there in the flimsiest pair of silk panties and some gravity-defying bra that only covered about half her breasts. She looked like she was going to spill out of it at any second, and it sure as shit didn't help that the damn thing was lacy and see-through.

With a dry mouth I muttered, "Get in."

She giggled. "I thought you were joining me."

Fuck. I *was* joining her, but I needed a second to get my erection under control. I climbed in after her, and the water hit us both. She peeled off her bra and revealed the most perfect pair of tits I'd ever seen in my life. Milky skin. Rose-tipped nipples. *Jesus H. Christ.* My imagination offered all the things I could do with breasts like hers. Hold them, weigh them, play with them, lick them...fuck them.

Shit, that was really not helping.

I just needed to get this done and touch her as little as possible.

I grabbed her sponge and handed it to her before squirting shower gel on it. "Start washing yourself."

Bailey made a face. "I want *you* to wash me."

Me too. But that wasn't going to happen.

"Bay, follow directions. I'll start with your hair." I found her shampoo, some raspberry-scented organic something or other. As a stream of water hit my back, I let it hit the back of her hair so the water would drench it. And that was when I noticed. She'd removed her underwear, too.

"Bay, what happened to your panties?"

She glanced at me over her shoulder and winked. "Well, I was wet."

I swallowed hard. "We're in the shower. We're both wet."

She shook her head. "That's not what I meant."

I. Was. So. Fucked.

I shampooed her hair as quickly as I dared, lathering and making sure it was nice and clean. I stepped aside, letting the spray drench her hair, and helping her rinse it out. All the while she kept lazily rubbing soap over her body. Jesus Christ, I wanted to help so badly, but that was a slippery slope.

Standing here, trying desperately to look at the ceiling while

I knew she soaped her tits, tested the limits of even my control.

Once her hair was rinsed out, I added the leave-in conditioner and gently worked it through her hair. She moaned, low and throaty, and my dick threatened to come without my fucking say so.

I could do this. I was the good guy. The sexually charged Hunter—the one who was demanding in bed, and got what he needed—I wasn't that Hunter when I was with her. Because I cared about her. I had to remember that.

After I gently took the brush through her hair from the tips to the roots as she instructed, she turned to face me, and I pinned my gaze directly over her shoulder and to the other side of the wall.

"Hunter, I just wanted to say thank you. Sorry I threw up."

I shook my head. "Not your fault. You had a hell of a trauma tonight. And so you overdid it. No big deal. We've all been there."

She pressed her body into mine and—what do you know?—my dick pulsed in my boxers. And then, ever so helpfully, Bailey rubbed her soapy tits on my chest. I let out a low groan that was part growl, and struggled with the reins of my control. But it wasn't until she wrapped her delicate hand around my boxer-clad cock that I lost it.

"Bailey, stop. One day soon, we're going to redo this whole scene. When that happens, I will have you turn that hot little ass around, plant your hands on the wall, and then I will bury my dick inside you. But right now is not that time."

She pouted, but she didn't release me. "But why not? You obviously want me."

"And you are obviously trying to get a spanking."

Her eyes fired wide, but her pupils also dilated. Well, well. It looked like Bailey was totally down for a spanking. Why did that make me want to give her one even more? Lucky for me, she wasn't too keen on listening. She shimmied and pressed her tits into me farther.

"Bailey. Last warning. You need to quit or you will feel my handprint on your ass."

"Hunter. I think I like this dominance in you." She kissed my chin and added a little slip of her tongue as a way to torment me.

I didn't mean to do it, but I couldn't help myself. I firmly set her away from me, turned her around and placed her hands on the opposing wall. Leaning over her back, my dick tented my boxers and pressed into the soft flesh of her ass.

When I whispered, my voice was low, "I warned you. Enough is enough." The crack of my palm over her ass surprised us both. She gasped, but then moaned low. The tingling started at the base of my spine.

No. No. No. I was not going to fucking come right now. Not okay. But I was walking away with one piece of knowledge tonight. Bailey Jones liked dominant Hunter. And I was done being a nice guy.

I took the little sponge and scrubbed myself off in seconds while I kept her in that position. I quickly washed down her back and legs, but at that point, my movements were perfunctory. In seconds, I had us both out of the shower. I wrapped us both in towels and left her briefly to go toss our clothes in the dryer.

When we had both toweled off, I marched her into the bedroom, and handed her a ratty T-shirt from her bottom drawer. I dragged it over her head before pulling back the covers and waiting for her to get in.

"Are you joining me?"

I shook my head even as my cock made an attempt to escape

the towel slung around my hips. "No. But don't worry, Bay, we're going to do this again real soon. And next time, I'm going to enjoy making your ass red. I promise I'll make sure to kiss it all better." I ignored her soft gasp and left her in the bedroom while I headed to the living room to watch TV and wait for my clothes to dry.

Once I was dressed again, I let myself out of her apartment. One good thing had come from tonight: now I knew exactly how to handle Bailey Jones.

Get WICKED now at malonesquared.com/wicked

ABOUT THE AUTHORS

NYT & USA Today Bestselling author **M. MALONE** lives in the Washington, D.C. metro area with her three favorite guys, her husband and their two sons. She holds a Master's degree in Business from a prestigious college that would no doubt be scandalized at how she's using her expensive education.

Independently published, her work has appeared on the New York Times and USA Today bestseller lists more than a dozen times. She's now a full-time writer and spends 99.8% of her time in her pajamas. **minxmalone.com**

USA Today Bestselling Author, **NANA MALONE**'s love of all things romance and adventure started with a tattered romantic suspense she borrowed from her cousin on a sultry summer afternoon in Ghana at a precocious thirteen. She's been in love with kick butt heroines ever since.

With her overactive imagination, and channeling her inner Buffy, it was only a matter a time before she started creating her own characters. Waiting for her chance at a job as a ninja assassin, Nana, meantime works out her drama, passion and sass with fictional characters every bit as sassy and kick butt as she thinks she is. **nanamaloneromance.net**